ALPHA WATCH

SAVANNAH'S FINEST SERIES

NICOLETTE JOHNSON

Day-N-Night Publishing

ISBN: 979-8-9852137-6-8

Library of Congress Control Number: 2023936517

Cover Photo 2023 www.authornicolettejohnson.com. All rights reserved-used with permission.

Author Photo 2022 InterSeeding Shutters Imagery, LLC. All rights reserved-used with permission.

PRINTED IN THE UNITED STATES OF AMERICA

❀ Created with Vellum

*The **STRUGGLE** you're*

in today

*is developing the **STRENGTH***

you need for

TOMORROW

—Unknown

PRELUDE

DOMINIQUE PARKER

"SHOTS FIRED! SHOTS FIRED!" Someone yells over the radio.

"Metro, we need officers now!" I howl into the radio, running towards the gunfire. Sarge sent us to Ellis Square to shut down the roadways early because the vehicular traffic is at a standstill. Within a matter of seconds, we hear gunfire ringing throughout the Entertainment District of Savannah.

"Metro, we have three down in City Market," another officer shouts into the radio.

"Metro copy. We're sending officers to you now!" Dispatch responds.

"Metro, officers been shot! I need EMS now!" I yell into the radio approaching the scene swiftly but cautiously with my duty weapon at a low ready. The injured officer is in my line of sight. I run towards the injured officer.

"Metro copy. Sending EMS now!"

"Oh, God," not Pierce. "Please, Pierce. Stay with me, baby. Please stay with me!" kneeling on my knees, embracing her head in my cradled arms.

"Metro, where the fuck is EMS? I need them now!" I scream over the radio.

"They're on their way!" Dispatch responds sternly.

Fuck it. I lift Pierce off the ground and throw her over my shoulder. "Stay with me, Pierce. Stay with me."

I place Pierce in the back of my squad car, and Ethan, my partner and best friend jumps in with her. I then run to the driver's side, throw on my emergency lights and sirens and haul ass to the hospital.

"Parker, she's not breathing, man."

"Start CPR. You got to keep her blood flowing."

Five minutes later, we arrive at the hospital. Ethan and I carry Pierce into the emergency room side entrance, where the nurses and doctors take over.

Yelling and screaming take over the radio. Another officer has been shot.

Another five citizens have been shot, making a total of ten people.

What in the world is going on in the City of Savannah?

CHAPTER ONE

DOMINIQUE

TWO YEARS LATER

ANOTHER FUCKING day in the City of Savannah where these assholes refuse to stop killing each other. What is it going to take for them to get their shit together?

Day after day and night after night, I sit in roll call and wonder why the fuck I even bother showing up anymore. Command staff always demanding shit from us, like we can actually stop these idiots from killing each other. The citizens of Savannah demand we stop harassing them, but they don't seem to give two fucks about their own people creating war in their backyards. They want to protest against White cops killing Black people, but they're the ones killing themselves.

March about that!

Raise hell about that!

Demand change for that!

We have ten people on this watch, and the only person I care to even speak to is Ethan, my partner. Noah Ethan is the pedigree of a Black man in the City of Savannah. At the age of twenty-five, dark-skinned, with short dreads, kept neat, you would think he'd be fucking broads left and right around here. But, no, he's just as sexually frustrated as I am. At least, that's what he complains about every damn day. He grew up with his White stepmother and three stepsisters, and half-sister. His father was killed in a car accident while patrolling the same streets we are in. His father was on the force for twenty years, leaving Ethan and his sisters with his stepmother.

I would have thought he and Sophie Martin would have hooked up, but I guess not. She sits in the corner of the squad room for every briefing. She's a light-skinned, short, thick, and a beautiful woman if you ask me. With those hazel eyes and short bobbed haircut, with tattoos up and down her arm, I would've hit that before, well, just before...

Then we have Victoria Morris. She's mixed with Asian and Black, bone straight black hair, with dark brown eyes. She has a passion for intelligence, and I can see her working closely with SARIC, our Savannah Area Regional Intelligence Center. But, unfortunately, she keeps mostly to herself, not really open with her personal life.

Gabriel Perez, sitting in the front, seems to have a thing for Morris but is too pussy to make a move. He's a Hispanic, possibly missed with White; who the hell knows. He has dark hair, kept long but off his collar, with piercing green eyes. He trained with the best of the best in the world before joining the department. Highly skilled in martial arts, he's the last person you want to fuck with when you're in a fight. I can see him heading to the Training Unit soon. They say he was a foster child and never knew his parents, so fighting for everything he had is an understatement.

Then there's Jackson Henry. The only White guy on our shift, well, besides sarge and the rookie. And boy, is he a true White boy with blonde hair and crystal blue eyes, standing six-four in height. A momma's boy, if you ask me. No kids, no responsibilities. As a matter of fact, his parents bought him a brand-new condo and drop-top

Mercedes for graduating with his master's. Rumor has it he is infatuated with our sistas. Hell, who wouldn't be.

Katherine Harris. What can I say? The darkest skin I've ever witnessed on a person, but boy, does it look good on her. She's short, thick, and athletically built. With short dark hair and pure grey eyes, there's been small talk about a stripper video of her out there. I haven't seen it, but with that body, I don't put it past no one. Katie is the partner of the apple of my eye, Harper Bradshaw. She just doesn't know it yet.

The other two officers are rookies. I never even bothered to get their name. I guess it's the prick in me.

Lieutenant Hall has been coming to our roll call for the past week, scouting and recruiting for his specialized unit. Where the fuck were they when I lost the love of my life, my best friend, my partner in crime? Huh, where the fuck was the Strategic Intelligence Unit then?

"Listen up," Sergeant McCloud announces. "Lt. Hall has something to say."

The squad room gets hushed the moment Sgt. McCloud speaks. That man has gained more respect from the frontline officers in the past two years than I thought he would. He has really stepped up after…

"Hey, ladies and gents. As you know, SIU has been scouting for new blood, fresh meat. We need, no, we want officers willing to give it their all and then some. SIU has brought down some real serious gangs, drugs, and human trafficking rings. But our job is never done. When we take one down, three more show up in their place. It's our job to stay three steps ahead of them. That said, if you're interested, reach out to your sergeant or me."

"Are there any questions?" Sgt. McCloud asks.

"Um, I have one," Harper Bradshaw speaks up.

Good God, she's sexy as fuck. With skin the smooth color of caramel, hair with curly ringlets pulled above her collar, and large dopey grey eyes and full lips, she can suck my dick any time of the fucking day.

But of course, can't go against my own fuck rule. Definitely can't go down that fucking road...not again.

"Yes, officer..."

"Corporal Bradshaw, sir."

"Yes, ma'am, go ahead."

"What are the minimum qualifications for the position?"

"I'm glad you asked Cpl. Bradshaw. We would want two years of experience, a go-getter, and a person with a passion for protecting the citizens of Savannah. We would like someone to have some experience in undercover work, but it's not necessary. We'll train."

"Thank you, sir."

"You're welcome. Anyone else?"

Crickets in the room. But then Lt. Hall glances my way as if waiting for me to say something. Man, fuck that. Ain't no fucking way I'm about to subject myself to foolishness.

"If that's it, I'll be on my way. Sgt. McCloud, thank you again for letting me crash your roll call."

"Anytime, bro, anytime."

Lt. Hall then walks out, and Sgt. McCloud releases us to our assignments.

FUCK! THAT FUCKING BITCH! KEISHA KEEPS DENYING ME MY son, Lucas. She was nowhere near this hateful when I met her all those years ago. As a matter of fact, she was the most pleasant person to be around until she started hanging out with those hood rats, putting garbage in her head about me fucking around on her.

She was the apple of my eye, smooth, dark-skinned, with curves that would knock you on your ass. Brown colossal eyes, short bobbed black hair, and a mouth made to suck dick.

I never even looked at another woman when I was with Keisha, not one. Now, she uses my son as a fucking pawn in her fucking game, and I hate it.

Me: Keisha, we agreed I would have Lucas every other weekend.

Keisha: Plans change…

Me: What the fuck Keisha. Lucas is my son too. You can't keep doing this. You can't keep him from me.

Keisha: I can, and I will.

"Fuck!" I roar out.

"Man, are you okay? What's going on?" Ethan asks.

Noah Ethan, my partner, has gotten me through plenty of shit over the years and helped me keep it together after Dayna was killed. He's a very private dude but cool as a fuck to chill wit. It took us a while to become friends, constantly butting heads on calls and shit, but when Dayna died, all that shit went out the window.

"Fucking Keisha," is all I have to say for him to understand.

"Dude, I told you what to do. You need to take her to court. This ain't right. She can't keep your son from you."

"I know, man. I've tried to do the right thing by her and Lucas."

"Well, it ain't working, so you must show her that you mean business."

"Twenty-two alpha one," dispatch raises over the radio.

"Twenty-two alpha one, go 'head," Ethan announces back.

"Domestic dispute at thirty-four East Jones Street. The girlfriend throwing complainant's clothes out the window, and now she is setting his clothes and car on fire. Fire and EMS enroute as well."

"Received. Twenty-two alpha one enroute," Ethan responds.

"Received," dispatch acknowledges.

"Dispatch, twenty-four alpha two will be enroute as well. We're right down the street," Bradshaw announces on the radio.

"Received," dispatch acknowledges.

Moments later, we arrive at thirty-four East Jones Street, and sure enough, a vehicle is engulfed in flames with clothes surrounding the car leading up to the home. Two kids about Lucas' age standing on the porch crying, and a female lying on the driveway with a male standing over her with a gun pointed at her head.

Ethan and I draw our weapons as we exit the vehicle. I see Bradshaw and Harris with their weapons out and giving verbal commands to the male to put his gun down. After a moment, I see Bradshaw holster her weapon and flank the suspect on his right. In a split second, she runs and kicks the gun out of the suspect's hand, then recovers to tackle him to the ground.

Ethan and I run towards her and assist her with handcuffing him, and then she handcuffs the female.

"What the fuck was that?" I spit out before I even know it.

"What do you mean?" Bradshaw questions, obviously confused at my outburst.

"You couldn't fucking wait on us? You had to save the fucking day all on your own?" I growl.

"First off, I have backup. Katie knew exactly what I was going to do. Second, you aren't my fucking keeper, so back the fuck off," Bradshaw spits out.

"Whoa, just a minute. Let's take care of these people first, and then we'll discuss the approach," Ethan interjects before I can respond.

"Fine, but I'm not done here."

"Well, I'm done," Bradshaw mutters.

"Hey guys, the kids can hear you. They are already scared to death, and they're about to lose both their parents. So please show some compassion," Harris speaks up.

Katherine Harris has been Bradshaw's partner for two years as well. She's attractive, but nothing compared to Bradshaw. Officer Henry always had a thing for her; he refused to act on it. Her demeanor is motherly, caring, and nurturing. Bradshaw, on the other hand, just doesn't give a shit. She's the tougher of the two. Almost like she had to be like that all her life.

We place the couple in separate vehicles while the fire department puts out the fire. Harris places the kids into her car while waiting on DFACS to respond. Ethan calls for a domestic violence investigator, and Sgt. McCloud.

Bradshaw takes custody of the weapon while Ethan gets the couple's information.

"Dude, you've got to calm the fuck down. You're taking your frustration out on everyone when the person you're really mad at is Keisha. Let's get through this shift and then have a drink afterward. You need one."

"You're right, man. I'm just so fucking pissed right now."

"I know, but take a beat. I got the rest of the night. Just type up the reports."

"Fine."

After riding a couple of calls, we all head back to the precinct to finish up our paperwork. Once in the precinct, I run into Bradshaw. Jesus, she smells fucking delectable. How is that even possible after working an entire shift?

"Uh, sorry. Didn't mean to bump into you. God knows we can't piss off the Hulk," she apologizes sarcastically, throwing up air quotes.

"What did you just call me?"

"The Hulk. You snap at a moment's notice, and we all have to just be okay with it. I don't know who pissed in your Wheaties, but you need to take a chill pill. No one is out to ruin your life," throwing her hands up, surrendering in defeat.

"Wow, is that what people are calling me now?"

"I'm afraid so, but I'm not scared of you."

"And you shouldn't be."

"I can't tell. You walk around like we owe you something."

"Well, hopefully, I can change that."

"We shall see."

She then walks away, swaying her hips from side to side. That uniform does no justice for her. I want to see what's underneath. Fuck, I need to stop. I need to get laid and soon.

CHAPTER TWO

HARPER BRADSHAW

"YES, FINALLY!"

"Congratulations Harper! Here are the keys to your new home."

"Oh my gosh. Thank you so much, Faith. You've been a godsend through this whole process."

Faith Richardson is a good friend and my realtor. She's been helping me find the perfect spot to build my dream home. I would have never acted on this build if it wasn't for her. So, not in so many words, I owe her so much.

"Of course, Harper. I should be thanking you. You've just made my quota for the whole year."

"Yeah, right," I respond in disbelief.

"I'm serious. This house is huge, and the commission will be beyond my beliefs."

"Okay, okay. I'm glad I could help. I needed the space. You know my dad is living with me, and I just needed room to live my life."

"I get it. Not everybody is like you. Most would've just put their dad in a home."

"You know why I couldn't do that."

"I know. I know. That's what makes you such a blessing."

"Anyways, I wanted something out of the city. Where I won't be bothered."

"Well, you've picked the perfect place."

"Thank you."

"Well, I must go, but please invite me to the housewarming party. I have the perfect gift."

"Fine, since you insist," rolling my eyes playfully. She knows I despise parties.

We both laugh, and she hugs me before getting into her car and driving away.

Oh my gosh! I did it! All that off-duty work paid off. I'm standing in front of my three-story home with a wrap-around porch and a yard to die for. My home is fully bricked in a greyish color with black shutters. I approach the door and insert my key for the first time.

I hear the lock click, and relief overwhelms me.

My home!

I enter the foyer and find stairs on both sides of the area leading to a loft on the second floor. Wooden floors spread throughout the home, and chandeliers overlooking each room. I walk towards the living area, and there's a kitchen to the right with a large island, bar area, and stainless-steel appliances. There is a goodie basket full of wine, cheese, fruit, and crackers.

"Faith's doing," I smile to myself.

I don't have any furniture yet, but I will soon. I had everything ordered last week, and it should be here tomorrow.

I head to the second floor where my father will be housed. There are four rooms on this floor, but he will have his own, equipped with a bathroom, and living room space, fully furnished tomorrow. I wanted him to have his own area where I won't feel like I'm hovering.

I then head to the third floor, where my sanctuary begins, with an office and bathroom housed, just for me. I have the entire floor, which I designed myself. It will be my favorite spot other than the gym on the first floor and the pool in the backyard.

I can't wait to make my home my own.

My phone rings, and I answer it. "Harper."

"Hi, Harper. It's Chip from Sey Hey. Your father, Ray, is here."

Joy ripped from me once again, "I'll be right over, Chip. Thanks for calling."

"Any time, Harper, but do know he got into a fight this time, and he's pretty banged up."

"Damnit, Daddy."

"I know. I know, just be careful. Don't get too worked up. Everything will be okay." I then hang up with Chip. But everything won't be okay. It's further from OK. Daddy has been getting overly wasted since momma left us. MaryAnn, my momma, left us when I was six years old. My daddy said she was such a beautiful soul, inside and out. I wonder what happened for her to just leave us like that.

The words she used when she left were, "Y'all are suffocating me. I can't breathe, and I need to be free."

How can a mother leave her only child and husband, who adored her with every fiber of their being?

How?

She has no idea what she's done to daddy and never will. I hate her for leaving me, for leaving us. I was fucking six. An impressionable young girl, full of dreams, hopes, and desires. And she just left us. My life changed forever that day. I lost my momma, and I lost my daddy.

Ray can only sleep or cope when he is completely obliterated. When he's sober, he just cries all day and all night. I've tried many times to get him clean and get him some help, but he refuses. And I don't want to leave him. I can't. He will die if I don't help him. So I just pray that one day, he will overcome this excruciating heartbreak.

I PULL UP TO SEY HEY WHEN I SEE MY DADDY HANDCUFFED IN the back of a squad car.

No, no, no. Please tell me Chip didn't call the police.

I get out of the car and approach the officers. Their backs to me. I tap one on the shoulder, and he spins around, catching him off guard.

"Parker?"

"Bradshaw, what are you doing here?"

"Um, well, Ray Bradshaw is my father. I've come to pick him up."

"Harper, I'm sorry. Someone in the bar called the police. I didn't know," Chip says apologetically, approaching very quickly. "I didn't know."

"It's okay, Chip. I understand," I assure Chip.

"Ray Bradshaw is your father? What are the fucking odds?" Parker spits out sarcastically.

"Please, just let me take him home. I promise he won't be a bother for the rest of the night."

"I don't think I can do that, Bradshaw. The vic wants to press charges."

"Parker, please. He won't survive jail," I beg.

After a while of contemplating, Parker walks away. Of all the fucking cops in the world, it had to be him to arrest my father. Fuck. There's no way he's going to look the other way on this one.

No fucking way.

Parker comes back to me after speaking with the victim, "The vic changed their mind after a little convincing; however, they want him to get some help."

"Yes, of course. I will make sure that happens first thing in the morning," I promise, a little surprised Parker would do something like that for me.

"That's not all. You're taking me to coffee at the Grind tomorrow, and we're going to chat about this. Understand?" And just like that, the fucking sentimental gesture, gone. Like it never even happened.

"Uh—"

"Nope, if not, the deal is off."

Giving in, "Fine, coffee," I agree, not really having any choice in the matter. He's such a dick. To use my dad's situation as a fucking pawn in his twisted game. God, I hate him.

"Good." He opens the back door of the squad car, letting my daddy out. "Mr. Bradshaw, you have an amazing daughter who cares about you. Be thankful she's willing to lay everything down for you. There aren't too many people left in this world like that."

"Right," my father slurs his response. "Best goddamn daughter in the world," he points out.

"Alright, daddy. Come on. We have a lot to talk about in the morning."

Parker helps me put him in my car, and I turn around, almost bumping into Parker. For the first time ever, I'm dangerously close to this man who has been an ass to me since I joined the force. He smells of whiskey, coffee, and sweat, three combinations that would drop any panties for him. Those eyes, hazel with a hint of gold flecks dancing before me, drinking me in thoroughly. I don't think I've ever witnessed him looking at me in such a seductive way. His breathing hitches oh so slightly, but I notice the change immediately. His stance towers over me, and for the first time, I see his strong muscular arms and large chest pulsating through his bulletproof vest. His curly brown hair is so alluring I just want to run my fingers through it.

"Hey, Parker."

Shit, he steps away with the mention of his name from Ethan, interrupting such a hypnotic moment.

Clearing his throat, "Yeah."

"I've already checked the cameras... oh, hey, Bradshaw. What are you doing here? I thought you were off tonight," Ethan asks, not noticing Parker's and I exchange. Thank the heavens above.

"Uh, Ray is my father."

"Oh... I see," Ethan draws out his words.

"Yeah, we all can't be so perfect, can we?" I blush with embarrassment, unsure if it's from my daddy's ridiculousness or Parker and I exchange.

"Oh, I didn't..." he tries to apologize for offending me, but I cut him off.

"It's okay. I got it from here. And Parker, thank you. I owe you."

Before he could answer, I jump into my car and pull away.

"What the fuck was that?" forgetting my daddy was in the backseat.

"Sorry, honey. I know I'm a disappointment. I promise to never do it again."

"Daddy, stop making promises you can't keep," I utter under my breath.

And just like that, he dozes off without another word.

I NEED A FUCKING DRINK AFTER THE FUCKED-UP DAY I'VE HAD. So once I get my father into bed, I dial Tommy's number. My go-to when I need to be broke off. The nigga knows how to fuck life into a bitch in need.

After four rings, I start to hang up, but that thick booming voice comes across the line, "Sexy five-O, how can I please you today?"

"Can you come over? I'm in need of your services."

"Damn, Five-O. You feening..." Tommy teases with a hint of sexual tension in his tone.

"You know it," I reply.

"Bet, I'll swing through in five. I got somewhere to be later."

"Fine by me."

We hang up, and I run into the bathroom to shower, shave my legs, and get this pussy right.

Ten minutes later, the doorbell rings; dad is in the room, passed out, and I'm about to release some much-needed stress, doggy style.

Story of my life once again.

CHAPTER THREE

DOMINIQUE

JUST WHEN YOU think you know a person, and bam, one simple revelation changes everything. Never in a million years would I have ever guessed Harper Bradshaw had skeletons in her closet. A drunk for a dad, who would have thought?

I wonder what else she got up her sleeve.

She always acts like she's better than everyone, not thinking through shit before she does it, and honestly, she is a fucking pain in my ass. But boy, would I like to have that ass bent over, stripped naked, and fucked roughly.

Maybe that's just what she needs, to be fucked thoroughly.

Fuck, I need to get laid to get that girl out of my head. I wonder if Lori is down for a quicky?

I send Lori a quick message before heading home.

I walk into my two-bedroom apartment at six in the morning, just getting off shift. I hate this fucking place, but it will have to do until I can get back on my feet. Fucking Keisha drained the very life I created out of my soul. She took everything from me and is now trying to take my son.

Well, fuck her. She will not take Lucas from me. Not ever.

I head for the fridge when I hear my phone ping. I glance at the screen expecting Lori, but no, it's Bradshaw.

Bradshaw: Are you ready for that coffee, or is it too early for you?

Shit, I forgot about our little deal to keep my mouth shut. I wouldn't have said anything, but she doesn't have to know that. I just love watching her squirm. The goosebumps spread across her arms, fist bawled at her side, and her eyes filled with lust made my dick twitch last night. Well, until Ethan interrupted our little exchange. Damn, that girl is doing something to my dick, something no one has ever been able to do.

Me: Sure! I can use coffee.

Bradshaw: See you soon. I'll be at the Grind waiting.

You sure fucking will. Bet, my new focus.

CHAPTER FOUR

HARPER

IT TOOK me all of ten minutes to get my daddy settled in his room in my apartment after breakfast. It's our last day here, and I have to take care of his drunk ass. He couldn't stay sober for one fucking day, so I can get the new house set up and ready to go.

Such a selfish prick. But I won't dare tell him that. I love him too much to hurt him even more than he already is.

Tommy did me a favor, taking all my frustrations away.

New focus, the pain between my legs, throbbing and getting rid of Parker's arrogant ass.

Parker is right though. I need to get my daddy some help; maybe now is the right time to do so. What if Chip didn't call me this time? He would have ended up in jail, and he would have never survived that.

I fucking begged, and I never beg for anything. I let my guard down in front of that asshole, and now I have to take him for coffee to keep his mouth shut. I never wanted anyone to ever have to witness the shit I go through every day. And for it to be that asshole. All the fucking people in this department, and it had to be fucking Parker. And now look, I'm doing the very thing I promised myself I would never do, beg.

He agreed to meet for coffee, so I change into a lovely summer dress and wear my curly hair down, insinuating my most attractive feature, my dopey grey eyes.

I've got to get him to keep his mouth shut, and the only way I can do that is to seduce him into submission.

I got this. I fuck men all the time; I just don't fuck men I work with, but what's the difference? He wants pussy just like any other straight man in Savannah. How hard could it be?

I ARRIVE AT THE GRIND, THE LOCAL HANG-OUT FOR COPS, dispatchers, and firemen. The quaint little shop is owned by Lt. Hall and his sister, Dianella. They wanted to create a place where law enforcement could hang out and not wonder if their coffee was being spit in or their food tampered with. The moment I walk in, my senses are attacked by the aromas of cakes, sweets, and freshly brewed coffee. There are industrial bar tops with stools, lounge sofas to relax, and bars to work at or just have a quiet moment from the world.

I grab a table in the back when I see Parker walking in with such authority and prestige. He's wearing a button-down olive-green shirt with black jeans, washed all so lightly and torn in different areas. His curly brown hair gives a playful mood to his sternness until he spots me in the back corner, and those dimples of his brighten the moment his eyes scan over me.

God, those dimples are every woman's wet dream. How did I not notice those dimples before?

I wave him over just when the waitress walks over to my table.

"Hi, I'm Jessie. What can I get you?"

"Um, I'll take a caramel macchiato with two shots of blonde espresso."

"Make that two," Parker says while taking a seat.

"Coming right up," Jessie says, then walks off.

"So, you trying to stay awake for the rest of the week, or you got something going on?" Parker inquires.

"The latter," I respond with no explanation. "I'm here to ensure you don't open your mouth about last night.

"And if I do, then what?"

"Just say you're gonna have a bad fucking day," I seethe.

"I doubt it, but it's cute how you think you can threaten me. I'll keep my trap shut if you have dinner with me."

"Look, you son-of-a-bitch, I agreed to coffee, not a fucking date...you know what, fuck this. I don't give a shit anymore," standing up, knocking the chair over as I retreat.

But I'm pulled and spun around into a hard chest. Parker steadies me on my feet, wrapping his hands around my wrist so I can't pull away.

"Just let me leave—"

"No, tell me what's going on, and I promise to leave my joking at the door."

I hesitate, shaking with pure anger and frustration. He is the last person on this fucking earth I want to talk to. "Sorry, I can't. Please let me go," I beg for the second time in my life.

He forces me to look into his eyes while he towers over me with his tall statue. I can see concern in his gaze, something I never witnessed before from this man. He's constantly fucking with me, so this, I can't phantom coming from him. Not him.

"Harper, please," and just like that, my walls vanquish completely. He has never called me by my first name. Never.

"Okay." He relaxes his grip on my wrists and guides me to sit back in his chair instead. Then he picks my chair back up and positions it next to me, giving me his undivided attention. "I...I don't—I don't even know where to start," I stamper over my words.

"How about the beginning," he offers.

Nineteen years of heartache and heartbreak, and he just wants me to drop it all in a couple of sentences over coffee. How delightful.

"Okay, here goes nothing," taking a deep breath. "My mother left my dad and me when I was six. She offered no explanation; she just left. Said we were suffocating her, or something like that, but whatever. My dad fell apart since then and can't function without a drink for more than a couple of hours. I've been taking care of him ever since. So there. That's all of it."

"You've been dealing with this all by yourself?"

"Yes," I respond incredulously. Who else will be there to help me?

"I ask because, well, do you have any other family that can help?"

"No," I snap. "Not that I know of," changing my tone. It's not his fault my family dynamics is shit. Taking a deep breath, "My mother was an only child and her parents died from what I was told, and my father's family kind of disappeared after he refused to answer any of their phone calls. So, it's just him and me, and I can't leave him. Not now, not ever."

"You need help, if not from family, then from professionals who specialize in alcoholism."

"I've tried that. My father refuses to cooperate with the facilities."

"I see. Why haven't you said anything before?"

"Seriously? You've treated me like shit for years, and the only reason I'm telling you now 'cause you're blackmailing me into a fucking date."

"Fair, I deserve that. I have been a little dickish."

"A little?" Raising my eyebrows.

"Okay, a lot. I've got shit going on, too, and I guess I've been taking it out on others."

"You, think?" rolling my eyes. "Sorry, that wasn't fair."

"Don't apologize. I deserve that."

"So, your turn," giving him the floor. I will not be the only one who pours their harrowing life story.

Jessie finally brings our coffee and offers some pastries that Dianella created. Anything she cultivates is mouthwatering. I will always be her taste bunny. "Thank you, Jessie. What has Dianella created this time?"

"Chocolate stuffed monkey bread. Be careful; it's messy."

"Oooh, I can't wait." I take a bite of the gooey greatness, and oh my goodness. It's heaven in my mouth, opening every bit of my senses. All of my frustrations melting into a puddle at my feet.

"Wow, did you just have an orgasm?" Parker stares at me.

"I think I did. You've got to taste this," shoving a mouth full into his mouth. Caramel dripping down the side of his lips, I swipe it with my finger without a thought in the world and lick my fingers clean. "Shit, I didn't—" obviously blushing three shades darker.

"It's fine, and you're right; this is delicious."

"Right. Dianella is an incredible baker. I love everything she creates."

"I can see that. I guess I know how to butter you up when I piss you off again."

"Yep, she's the key to my heart."

"You don't say."

"Enough trying to change the subject. It's your turn, now spill the beans," taking another bite of my monkey bread.

And we both burst out laughing, like an ugly belly, roll-over laugh.

"Okay, okay...I have an ex from hell who has drained everything from me, and now she's keeping me from my son," pausing, "I think that sums it up."

"Shit. You got it worse than me."

"Yep, I'm afraid so."

"What are you going to do?"

"I'm taking Keisha to court."

"Keisha?"

"Yeah, Keisha Parker, my ex-wife."

"Wow," taking another gulp of my coffee. "We are a couple of fucked up people, aren't we?"

"Speak for yourself. I'm perfectly fine."

"Yeah, right. Whatever you say," rolling my eyes.

We finish our coffee and monkey bread and continue to make small talk, something we haven't done since I joined Alpha Watch two years ago. This just might be a breakthrough for both of us. Wait until I tell Katie. She is going to freak.

After fighting over the tab, we head to our separate vehicles.

"I wasn't joking about dinner. I would love to take you out sometime," Parker says as I open my car door.

"Oh, I don't date guys I work with."

"And if I didn't work with you?"

"Then, just maybe I will give you a slight chance," measuring with my fingers for emphasis.

"Then I guess I need to make some changes."

"Don't go quitting your day job over me."

"Me, of course not," he says sheepishly.

"Thank you."

"Thanks for what?"

"Thank you for listening. I needed it and didn't even know it. Now I must unpack my shit and wait for the movers at my new place."

"Oh, you just moved?"

"Not yet. The movers are coming over today. I just had a home built in the Highlands. Wanted to get out of the city, yet still, be in the city if that makes sense."

"Perfect sense. Do you need any help?"

"No, I think I got it. Just needed caffeine to get me going. Anyways, until next shift."

"Likewise. And the offer is still there if you need it."

"I appreciate it. Thanks."

I then climb into my car and drive away before I change my mind. I never witnessed this side of him. He can be very charming. Something I didn't know was even possible. He's always so angry, but now I know why. Hopefully, this is a good sign for the future.

CHAPTER FIVE

DOMINIQUE

"KEISHA, OPEN THE FUCKING DOOR," I continue banging like a madman. This crazy bitch has locked me out of my own fucking house. I can't see my son, and now she's ignoring my phone calls.

The gall of this hoe.

As soon as I left the Grind, I drove straight here to see my son, "Keisha, I'm not going to say it again." The door then flies open; a stocky dude stands before me, fist balled up. "Where's Keisha?"

"She ain't your concern no mo. So, step."

"I ain't going nowhere until I get my son."

"My nigga..."

"I ain't yo nigga, so step aside, or I'll make you." This joker needs to get the fuck out my face. "Listen, all I want is my son. I don't give two fucks who Keisha is fucking with. Just hand over my son."

"Little nigga, get down here," he barks over his shoulder.

Jesus, give me strength. I'm two seconds from losing my shit.

"Lucas," I yell through the open door.

Lucas comes flying down the stairs at full speed. Tears streaming down his face. He crashes into my embrace, knocking me back a little.

"Hey, man, it's okay. Daddy's here."

"Daddy, please get me out of here. Mommy left me here with this guy, and he scares me," Lucas cries out.

The dude chuckles as he slams the door shut.

"It's okay. We're leaving now." I grab my son and head for the car, not giving a shit where Keisha is or the nigga she got in my house. I am so fucking done with her.

As Lucas and I enter my apartment, I ask him if he's eaten. He hasn't said a word on the ride over.

"Daddy, can I go to my room? I'm not ready to eat yet."

"No problem. We're having seafood mac & cheese and fried chicken, your favorite," I say enthusiastically. But it doesn't cheer him up. I'm almost fucking afraid to ask him what happened because just the slightest hair disturbed on his body, and I will fucking lose it.

"Okay, daddy. I just want to play FortNite for a little while, and then I will help," he says with absolutely no emotions. Fuck, I hate seeing him like this.

My boy is full of life and happiness. He's never had to deal with failure or heartache, and it's ripping me apart knowing his mother has put him in such a horrible predicament.

It's crazy how a person can change so much within a year span. Keisha was so devoted to us, our son, and our family, and when I joined the force, all of that changed. She started hanging out with these women, who, of course, were single, and I just think Keisha wanted to experience that part of life. We were together for so long. I just wish she would have talked with me. I would've given her the world if she asked.

I joined the force for us. I wanted to provide a stable life for her and Lucas. I never wanted to take her individuality from her, not ever. Such a brilliant and beautiful soul, just gone. Now what sits in her place is a wicked, selfish, manipulative heartless bitch. So cold and ruthless. Her sister, Raquel, told me she started doing drugs, lost her job, and pretty much living off of the child support I pay. She's behind on the house and headed into foreclosure in a month.

Everything we've worked so hard for, gone.

I decided to call my divorce lawyer to get advice on full custody of Lucas.

"Dominique, from what you've told me, you have a strong case against your ex-wife. Now, I'm not saying it will be easy, but it's definitely promising."

"That's good news. Finally, something I've needed to hear all day," I sigh.

"We can file for an emergency temporary custody order until the court date. That means Lucas will stay with you until we go before a judge. Is that something you're willing to do?"

"Yes, of course. Look, my son was left with a stranger for God knows how long, and when I picked him up, he was physically and emotionally depleted. I've never seen my son like that, ever. So I must do whatever it takes to get my son back to normalcy."

"Perfect, I'll file the paperwork today and will call you when it's complete."

"Thank you, Marissa. I truly appreciate all of your hard work on this case."

"No problem. It's my job. Keep your phone near you. I'll call with an update as soon as I get one. In the meantime, you might need to go somewhere Keisha can't find you. At least for a couple of days. I'm hoping I can get this done sooner than later, but you never know."

"Okay, I'll see what I can do." We then say our goodbyes and hang up.

I decide to head to Lucas' room to check on him. "Hey buddy, you mind if I play with you."

"Sure," handing me the other remote, he adds me as a secondary player.

"So, fill me in on Lucas' World." This is something we both came up with when I started working the force so I wouldn't miss out on anything in his life. I got the idea from Bobby's World, a TV show I watched all the time growing up.

"Um, what do you want to know?" he asks hesitantly.

"Everything, of course."

"Daddy, what happened to mommy?" the question hit me like a brick slamming right into my gut with such force, nearly knocking me completely out. But I hold it together for this impressionable young boy.

"What do you mean?" I ask carefully, trying to come up with anything to say to him.

"I haven't seen her in four days. She left me with that guy and said she would be right back. Then she took my phone, so I couldn't call you. I was so scared," he quipped with so much anguish.

"Oh, man. I had no idea. It was mommy's turn to be with you. If I'd known, I would..." not able to finish that sentence, anger ripping through my veins. I'm trying so fucking hard not to go kill that bitch. How could she leave our son like that? How? What fucking mother does that to her child? "It's going to be okay. I got you, buddy. Everything will be just fine," I promise him, and I intend to keep my promise. If it's the last thing I do.

CHAPTER SIX

HARPER

"DADDY, it's time to get up and eat something. We have a long day ahead of us," I announce softly as I walk in and open the blinds to his room to let in some much-needed light. "Daddy?" I call again when he doesn't answer.

I don't hear him stir, so I rock him gently. "Daddy, it's time to wake up." When he doesn't budge, fear starts to creep up my spine. I check his pulse, praying that I can find one.

It's very faint, but there's one. I grab my phone from my back pocket and dial 9-1-1.

"911, what is your emergency?"

"It's my father. He's not waking up, but he has a feeble pulse."

"What is your name, ma'am?"

"Harper Bradshaw. My father's name is Ray Bradshaw."

"Harper, this is April in dispatch."

"Oh, hi, April. Please send an ambulance to 508 Indian Street. I'm in apartment 85 on the top floor."

"We're sending them now. Harper, do you remember the new CPR I taught you in training last week?"

"Yes," I sniff.

"Okay, if you lose a pulse, I need you to roll your father on his back on the floor and do chest compressions just like I taught you. We're no longer doing mouth-to-mouth."

"Okay. April?"

"Yes, honey?"

"I'm so scared."

"I know you are, but I'm right here. I'm not leaving you."

Moments later, I hear loud banging on the door. I unlock the door with the app on my phone and tell them to enter through the ring camera doorbell.

"I'm back here," I bellow, soon after I hear several people in my apartment.

"Harper?"

"Katie...oh Katie. My daddy...I—," I begin, but can't finish the sentence through sobbing.

"It's okay, sweetie. We got it from here," Katie pulls me into a loving embrace. "Sarge told me to stay by your side, so I'm here for whatever you need, okay?"

I nod and physically break down while EMS works on my dad.

"Bradshaw?"

I turn around at the mention of my name. That voice. It can't be him. He's off today, isn't he? I've been so lost in everything; I can't even remember what day it is.

"Yes?"

"What medication is your dad on?"

"Uh, um, it's in my phone; hold on. I have a calendar for the times and what meds to take," handing over my phone to Parker, too frantic to search through my phone.

"That's perfect. Thank you," Parker responds with an underlining tone I don't recognize. Is that empathy he's giving off in his demeanor? It can't be.

"Harper, sweetie, let me take you back to my house. We can binge-watch Grey's Anatomy, drink wine, and eat junk food."

"I would love that, but I have to meet the moving crew at my new house. This is the second time I've had to reschedule, and I can't do it again."

"Okay, why don't I go with you?" Katie offers.

"You don't—"

"I know, but I want to," she interrupts me. "Besides, Sarge is keeping me on the payroll. So I'm free to do whatever you want on the City's dime." We both burst out laughing.

"What's so funny?" Parker, Ethan, and Martin ask.

"How does a moving party sound?" Katie shouts.

Everyone looks at each other and then me. Like I'm the deciding factor or not.

"Guys, you really don't have to do this," I whine through laughter and sobs.

"We know. But we will."

"Then, it's settled. Call Gab, Jackson, Perez, and Morris. Party at Harper's. I'll bring the food. Parker and Ethan, can y'all grab the booze? Everyone else, bring your muscles," Katie starts barking out orders, and everyone follows suit.

I love these guys. They have really become the family I never had.

EMS wheels my father away, and reality slams into me like a dump truck. This may be the last time I see my father, and once again, I fall apart surrounded by my true family, Alpha Watch.

A COUPLE OF HOURS LATER, MY DAD WAS PRONOUNCED deceased at the hospital. I didn't have the strength to make it there. Really because I just didn't want to see him like that. I'm convinced he died of a broken heart, like, seriously, a broken heart. My dad loved my mother so much every organ in his body shut down, and it was too late to save him from his heartbreak.

I just want to remember my daddy as the man I knew eighteen years ago, loving, caring, and full of life. He was always smiling, telling jokes, and God, did he love my momma. He loved her so much it killed him.

Katie drives me to my new home, and just the expression on her face gives me life.

"What in the world are you going to do with all of this space?"

"I don't know. I had it built for my daddy and me. Now, it's just me."

"You can always rent a room. I heard Ethan talking the other day about Parker needing to find a place for him and his son. If you offer it to him, he may take you up."

"Seriously, Dominique Parker living with me? Are you crazy? He hates me."

"I wouldn't be so sure about that. I see the way he looks at you."

"You mean the way he wants to slice my throat?"

"Whatever, it was just a suggestion. You would be doing him a huge favor. His ex-wife is bat-shit crazy."

Piquing my interest, "How crazy?" Dominique told me a little, but not much.

"Let's just say she sold their son for a week for drugs and then disappeared for another two weeks."

"Shit. I had no idea."

"Yeah. She has really changed since high school."

"Y'all went to school together?"

"Yep. Those two were inseparable in high school and in college. Then she started partying really hard and just don't give a shit anymore."

"Wow. That's so sad."

"Tell me about it. Oh, and I told him he could bring his son. Unfortunately, he couldn't find a babysitter. I hope that was fine."

"Uh, yes, of course," agreeing to everything because I feel numb.

"I told my sister to bring my niece and nephew. They're the same age as Lucas."

"Totally fine. I have a game room and a huge backyard they can play in."

"See, you're already prepared for a roommate with kids," she flashes me a devilish smile.

"We shall see," rolling my eyes. "He might not even take the offer. He hates me, remember?"

"That man loves you, and I'm willing to bet he'll have you bent over the table, fucking your brains out, and you calling his name by the end of the week."

"Seriously, Katie. What kind of girl do you think I am?" slapping her on the arm.

"Don't give me that innocent girl shit. I've seen you in your prime. Just wait. And when it happens, you owe me a box of salted cameral chocolates and lunch," she adds.

Rolling my eyes, "Just park the damn car.

Everyone pulls up at the same time, parking in my large driveway.

"Wow, Bradshaw. This is a sweet piece of property," Ethan whistles.

"Thanks. I've saved every penny from off-duty to build it. I just wish my daddy could have seen my hard work."

"Oh, he sees it. Just up there," Parker points to the open sky.

I blush at the sentiment. "And this must be Lucas. It's nice to meet you. I'm Harper. I work with your daddy."

"Cool. You're a cop too?" Lucas gushes.

"Yep. We all are, well, except for Victoria Morris over there. She's our analyst, but she might as well be a part of the crew," Victoria waving at the little ones.

"Wow, that's so cool. Dad, can I go play with the other kids?" Lucas asks anxiously.

"Yeah, buddy. No horsing around."

"Okay, dad," Lucas yells over his shoulder, running at full speed.

"He's a very well-mannered young man you got there," I compliment, standing back up.

"Yeah, I try my best. Don't want him to become a statistic."

"I don't blame you on that one. That's why I built my home on the outskirts. I don't want to raise my family in Savannah anymore. It's just too much going on."

"I get it."

"Here, let's head in. First, I have to direct the movers where I want everything, and we just have to set it up."

"Well, put me to work. I'm here for whatever you need," he says with conviction in his tone, and I think I hear a little seduction and humor as well. But I push that thought away. Katie is far from the truth regarding Dominique Parker and me.

CHAPTER SEVEN

DOMINIQUE

WHILE TOTING one of Bradshaw's dressers to the second floor, my phone rings. I've been waiting on this call all week. I set he dresser down and answer the phone.

"Parker."

"Hi Dominique, I have great news. You have temporary full custody until the court date, which is four weeks from Monday. After that, you will have to show a stable home for Lucas. I know you already have that, so the hard part is done."

"Thank you so much. You have no idea how much this means to me," I physically sigh, lifting about fifty pounds off my shoulders, not including the dresser I just carried.

"Oh, I think I know. Get your finances and home in order, and you should be good. A case worker may come by to check how everything is going. Let them."

"Gotcha. Is there anything else I need to do?"

"Send me your current address soon so I can hand it over to the courts and the case worker, and that should be it."

"Okay," I answer, physically tensing all over again. Unfortunately, I haven't found a suitable place just yet, and I'm running out of time.

We then disconnect.

"You haven't found a spot yet, have you?" Ethan asks.

"Naw, and time is running out. Everything I can afford right now is shity as fuck. I can't raise my son in those mold-infested rundown shit holes."

"I feel you, man. If I had the space, y'all could crash at my place."

"I know, man. I know. It just saddens me that this may make or break my custody issue with Keisha," I respond with defeat in my tone. Something I don't even recognize.

We head back downstairs when I almost knock Bradshaw clean off her feet. I have to grab her to steady her from falling down the stairs.

"Shit, sorry, Bradshaw. I didn't see you."

"It's okay. I'm fine. I just—"

"Yeah?" I ask because she seems to have something on her mind.

"I wanted to talk to you about something. Do you have time right now?"

"Sure, go ahead, Ethan. I'll meet you downstairs in a few." I turn back to face Bradshaw, those gorgeous eyes holding my gaze. "Whatcha need?"

"I have a proposition for you if you're willing to hear me out."

"Shoot." What in the world could she possibly offer me.

"I hear you're looking for a place for you and your son, and I no longer have my dad living with me, and I was hoping if you're interested that y'all could stay with me, well, of course until you're able to find something permanent. But, I mean, if you want to or haven't found something, I mean—" she rambles on.

"Bradshaw," cutting her off. "Slow down."

"Yes, sorry. I ramble when I'm nervous."

"Clearly."

"I have this six-bedroom home, and it's just me. I'm offering you a place to stay until you're able to find something of your own. I trust you more than a stranger living here, so what do you say?" she announces with a little more confidence.

"I don't know what to say. You've caught me completely off guard. I wasn't expecting this at all. Hell, I didn't even know you knew I was looking."

"Yeah, Ethan mentioned it to Katie and Jackson, and of course, Katie mentioned it to me, or Katie heard it from Ethan, whatever. So, what do you say?"

"If I do this, I want to help with half of everything. And my son is very well-mannered. You won't even know he's here. And I have a babysitter for him on days we are working."

"Of course. I wasn't worried about any of that, and I know you wouldn't mind helping if I needed it. You'll actually be doing me a favor. So, we gotta deal?"

She extends her hand out and has no idea what she's done. She's my absolute guardian angel right now, my savior. Pulling her into a hug, because a handshake isn't enough. I know I've caught her off guard as she tenses in my embrace. But I don't give a shit. She saved Lucas and me. "Bradshaw, you have no idea how much this means to me. I owe you everything."

"You owe me nothing. When you're ready, here are the spare keys; I have automatic locks, so I will send you the door and alarm app. You both will be on the second floor. All the rooms have their own bathroom, so you will have your privacy," she offers firmly.

"Thank you!" is all I muster up right now. She has ultimately saved me from that crazy bitch.

"Whenever we have time, we can discuss everything over drinks or that dinner you've been trying to get me to have," she laughs.

"Who knew all I had to be is homeless for you to finally give in?" I shrug my shoulders.

"Right, I guess I'm a sucker for homeless guys and drunks," she says sarcastically and breaks down right in front of mc.

"Shit, I didn't mean—"

"Stop. Please stop apologizing," sobbing loudly, Harper continues. "It's not your fault my dad died. I just miss him so much, even though it's only been a couple of hours. Y'all have really done so much to keep my mind off everything."

"I meant what I said earlier. I'm here no matter what."

"I know you are." She slips from my embrace, and we both head downstairs to join the rest of the team.

For the most part, we've got all the boxes in the critical areas. Now, we just have to unpack everything.

AFTER ABOUT SIX HOURS OF UNPACKING AND LUCAS RUNNING himself ragged, we head to my apartment to pack our things. I don't have a whole lot, which is perfect because Bradshaw has everything imaginable. She thought of everything.

I pull up into the complex and find a parking space. When I get out of the vehicle, Keisha and that same guy that was at her house approaches me.

Come on. Give me a fucking break. Just once.

"Give me my son back, you asshole," Keisha spits out without warning.

Lucas is sleeping in the backseat, so he won't witness the shit that's about to go down.

"Where the fuck have you been, Keisha?"

Ignoring my questions, "Give me my son back, or I will fucking kill you!" she threatens.

"I have full custody now. So, you and homeboy can go fuck yourselves." I turn to get back into my car when I feel a hand on my shoulder. Before I know it, I've been spun around and dodging a knife heading straight for my gut by the dude with Keisha. As my fist impacts with his face, Keisha tries to stab me as well, but she ends up stabbing buddy in the side.

He falls with a hard thud. She then cries out in disbelief as he collapses on the ground. People start coming out of the apartment, and Keisha starts yelling, "He stabbed him for no reason. How could you do that?" Pointing her finger at me.

Staring in utter disbelief, one of my neighbors speak up. "He didn't stab him, you did, and we got it on camera."

I can see the black coldness in her eyes; trembling with fear, Keisha then stumbles over the curve, looks around, and then takes off running, leaving her boy toy to bleed out in the parking lot.

"Don't worry, we've called 9-1-1, and we have everything on video. We saw the whole thing," another elderly neighbor says. And, man, am I glad I have neighbors who don't mind speaking up.

Speaking out.

I drop to my knees to put pressure on the stab wound of the boy toy. "Hey buddy, can you give me your name?"

"Fuck you," he spits out.

"I'm trying to help you. First, however, we need to know who you are to give to the authorities," I seethe.

"I'm going to kill you and that bitch."

"Not if I let you bleed the fuck out."

"Fuck you."

"Son, you don't want to do that. Think of your son and your career," someone whispers in my ear. Debating with my inner thoughts to not fucking let this son-of-a-bitch bleed to death, I hear sirens in the distance, and I snap back to reality.

"Lucas!"

"I've got him," one of the female neighbors confirms. "I've got him."

"Thank you." I manage to stand to my feet and wait. And just wait.

"Parker, is that you?" I hear Lt. Hall asks as he walks through the crowd that gathers around me and boy toy.

"Yes, sir. It's me."

"What happened? Are you okay?" he asks, looking me over, probably because of all the blood I have on me.

"L.T. I—I don't know where to start. Fuck, it happened so fast."

"Here, come with me," L.T. guiding me from the crowd.

"Wait, my son."

"You have a son?"

"Yes, sir."

"Shit, I had no idea. Where is he?"

"He's right over there," I point to one of my neighbors.

"Okay, I will have Officer Jones get him. He's really good with kids."

"I don't want him leaving my side."

"He'll be right by your side. But you must tell me everything. Start from the beginning."

"I've gotten a divorce from my wife, Keisha because she started doing crazy shit over the past three years or so. She's been giving me a hard time about my son and visitation. So, earlier today I went over to our— her home and found this guy," I pointed to buddy on the ground. "at my—Keisha's house. He was there alone with my son, and my son won't talk about it, but I know that dude did something to him. Keisha has been M.I.A. for over three weeks, so I filed for temporary full custody through my lawyer and won. I was headed back to my place to pack some things because I knew she would lose her shit when she got the news. When I arrived here, they were waiting for me. They then tried to stab me, and in doing so, Keisha stabbed buddy in the side. She then tried to blame it on me, but my neighbors got the whole thing on camera. She took off running when confronted with that information, leaving him on the ground. And that's all of it."

"Okay, get your son and whatever you need from the apartment. We got it from here. I'll call you if I need anything else."

"Yes, sir." I head over to my son, and he runs and jumps in my arms, holding my neck as tight as his little arms will allow.

"Daddy, are you okay?"

"Yes, buddy, I'm okay. Are you?"

"That man did that to me too."

"Did what?" piquing my interest.

"Dug the knife into my side. It hurt so bad. Did it hurt you?"

Gapping with fiery lava in my blood, my temp rising to levels not possible, and my vision blurring as I grip my son in my arms.

"He—he did what?" I seethe between labored breaths.

"He poked me with that knife. I'm okay, though, daddy. No need to worry. I'm strong, just like you," he flexes his arms to show me his muscles.

"That you are. Come on, buddy. Let's grab a night bag. We're staying at Bradshaw's house."

"Really?" He asks with enthusiasm, forgetting our previous conversation. I haven't spoken to him about moving, so I don't know how he's going to take it. "Harper's house is cool. She got a pool and everything. Oh, man, I can't wait." He hops out of my arms and dashes into the apartment.

I guess he'll be cool with it.

By the time I reach the front door, Lucas has his bookbag full of toys and his gaming system hanging out the top.

"What about your clothes?" I question with amusement in my tone.

"I'm getting that next!"

"Okay, buddy. Be careful with everything. That PS5 is expensive."

"Yes, sir." He then starts tip-toeing, moving incredibly slowly. He has no idea how much he cheers me up sometimes. "Do you think Harper likes playing games?"

"Can't hurt to ask but hold on just a minute. I need to talk to you."

"Okay." He sits on the edge of the couch, waiting in anticipation.

"So, Harper offered us to live with her for a while until we can find something a little bigger. How do you feel about that?"

"That's awesome."

"Now, we must be on our best behavior, keep our room clean, and help Harper out as much as possible. We don't want her to regret allowing us to stay, okay?"

"Yes, sir. I will be a big boy and help as much as possible."

"That's my boy! And we do our secret handshake.

We finish packing our stuff and put everything in the trunk area of my car. I don't have a massive vehicle, but it fits everything we need for now. We then drive over to Bradshaw's, praying I don't fuck this up for her, Lucas, or me.

Number one rule, keep my dick in my pants.

CHAPTER EIGHT

HARPER

I HEAR KNOCKING on my door, so I head downstairs to answer it. It's Parker and Lucas standing there with luggage trailing behind.

"Hey guys, you could have used your key or the code."

"I didn't want to scare you."

"Valid point. I've been extremely jumpy lately." I step aside, letting them in, "Here, come in."

They walk past me, and I get a whiff of Parker's cologne, and it damn near brings me to my knees. Jesus, he smells so good, a perfect combination of whiskey and coffee. Shit, down, girl.

I guide them to the second floor, where I've made up their rooms. "Wow, you've been busy."

"Yeah, I clean when I'm uneasy, frustrated, bored, or whatever."

"Want to talk about it?" He asks.

"No, not right now," I offer before Lucas interrupts me.

"Hey, where's my room?"

"Lucas, what did we talk about?" Parker chastises.

"Be on our best behavior and help Harper out," Lucas bows his head in defeat.

"That's Ms. Harper to you, okay?"

"Yes, sir. Sorry, Ms. Harper."

"It's okay, Lucas. Your room is right down here." So I guide them to Lucas' room, and his face lights up when he enters.

"This is my room?" he drags out.

"Yes. All yours."

"Wow, this is awesome. There are so many toys and video games, and you bought me clothes too?"

"You didn't have to do that, Bradshaw?" Parker confesses.

"I know. I wanted to. Besides, y'all been through enough already."

"You don't know the half of it."

"Yeah, the bad man tried to poke daddy like he poked me."

I look up at Parker, mainly because he's six foot three and I'm five foot four, but what in the world is Lucas talking about? Thoroughly confused.

"I'll tell you once I get Lucas settled," he promises me more so with those dreamy, seductive eyes.

Goddamnit Harper. Get it together. Ain't no way you fucking this man. Roommates, and that's it.

"Okay, I've already cooked dinner. I hope y'all like fried fish and grits smothered in gravy, onions, and peppers."

"We sure do," Lucas announces while playing with all the toys.

"Yes, thank you, Bradshaw."

"Stop calling me Bradshaw. We're not working. It's Harper."

"Okay, then it's Dominique to you as well."

"Fair." I then leave the room and let them have some alone time before dinner.

WE'RE ALL SITTING AT MY NEWLY BUILT ISLAND, EATING FISH and grits, and having a good time. I'm thrilled I decided to let them stay. I really needed them around, whether they realized it or not.

Lucas is such a precious boy, full of life and wonder. He's so inquisitive and observant. He has eyes like his daddy, hazel with flecks of gold shining at times. He's slightly darker than his father but just as handsome. He's gonna break plenty of hearts when he gets older.

It's crazy how Dominique and I have gotten so close these past couple of weeks. Hell, he wouldn't say two words to me for two years; now, we hold complete sentences and laughing and shit.

Lucas starts swaying in his chair, knowing damn well he's tired but trying to hold on for dear life in hopes of not missing anything.

"Okay, buddy. Time for bed."

"Ah man, no, daddy. I'm not sleepy."

"Please, boy, yes, you are. Now let's hit the sheets. Tell Ms. Harper good night."

"Good night, Ms. Harper," Lucas pouts.

"Good night, buddy. If you head to bed now, we can get in the pool tomorrow afternoon. How does that sound?"

He perks up and takes off for the stairs.

"Thank you," Dominique mouths.

"Of course. I meant what I said. Pool party tomorrow."

Dominique smiles, "I'll be right back."

"Okay." He heads upstairs, and I pour myself a glass of wine for a nightcap. It's been an emotional rollercoaster of a day, and I just want to kick back and relax. I'm still trying to get used to my new home. The captain gave me time off to grieve my father, but there's so much that has to be done and not enough time in the day to do everything. And crying isn't on the to-do list.

The lawyers called today, wanting me to come by. It hasn't even been twenty-four hours, and the vultures are in full effect. I haven't mustered the strength to go there. It seems so final to go over everything, and I'm not ready for that just yet.

Dominique strolls downstairs looking breathtakingly beautiful and haven't changed a thing about himself. Shit, it got to be the wine fucking with my vision because I ain't neva want to fuck someone so bad it hurts. Neva.

"Hey, sorry about that. He's always trying to stay up like he's gonna miss something."

"No, worries. He's such a breath of fresh air. Kids brighten everything. Hey, do you want a glass or something a little stronger?"

"Something a little stronger. It's been a fucked-up day," and with that revelation, it brings me back to the comment Lucas made earlier.

"I've got whiskey, gin, tequila, bourbon, you name it, I got it."

"How on earth do you have a fully stocked bar already?"

"I work off-duty at Habersham Beverage. So I get discounts," I stroll over to the bar, plastering a massive grin on my face.

"Makes sense. I'll take whiskey. It's crazy how I know nothing about you, and we work with each other every day."

I pour two fingers into my brand-new crystal glasses. "Well, you were too busy fucking with me to notice." There's a whole lot he hasn't noticed about me.

"Well, that's certainly going to change now," handing him the glass, and he takes a large gulp. Looks like we're going to need the whole damn bottle. I head back and grab it, setting it on the coffee table. "Wow, that's good. What is that?"

"It's Ghost Coast honey whiskey."

"That's smooth, with an excellent flavor. Never had it."

"Ghost Coast is a local brewery in Savannah. I'll have to take you there sometime."

"I'll certainly hold you to that," he smirks with that panty-dropping smile.

"I'm sure you will," needing to change the subject. It's getting heated in here. "So, bad day, hun."

"You have no idea," shoving his free hand through his messy curls.

"Enlighten me," taking a deep breath and another swig of his drink, he begins with his story.

"Well, for starters, my ex-wife and her boy toy tried killing me today and kidnapping my son in the process. Jokes on her."

Spitting out all of my wine all over the place, "What?"

"Yeah, they tried to ambush me at my apartment after leaving here earlier. That crazy bitch disappeared for weeks, and then she just shows the fuck up, demanding I give her my son. When I refused, her boy toy tried stabbing me first, and when he failed, she tried, but she ended up stabbing him instead. What a fucking joke," he spits out while I clean up my mess. Thank goodness I switched to white wine.

"So, did she... you know, kill him?" I question.

"Nope, but boy, did I want to. It took my neighbor to talk me off the ledge because I was two seconds from gutting that bitch to death with his own knife. Then Keisha fucking ran off after another neighbor said they captured the whole incident on camera."

"Wow, so when Lucas said...."

"Yeah, the fucker was jabbing my son in the side with a knife, antagonizing him. That's why he was so standoffish lately. I knew something happened; I just didn't want to force him to come clean. I wanted him to tell me on his own. And boy, when he did...just say, that bitch better be glad she ran off. I don't know what I would have done if she hadn't," he admits.

"Don't beat yourself up. You're human. Any other person would have had the same thoughts."

"I know, but we're cops. We are held to a higher standard."

"Like I said, we're human too. Your son's life was in danger. No one would have blamed you for protecting your son."

And now, it's my turn to comfort him as he slowly breaks down in front of me. I set my wine glass down and take his glass out of his hand. I wrap my small arms around his broad shoulders and try my best to soothe his pain.

"Lucas is my life. God, if anything happens to him..." not finishing the sentence. I know exactly what he means at this moment.

"We won't lose him. He has us both. We'll protect him at all costs."

"We?" Lifting his head in disbelief, he questions me as if he's hearing something other than what I stated.

"Yes, we," I confirm with every fiber in my being. I could never let anything happen to a child, especially Lucas. And before I can pull away, Dominique's full soft lips are on mine, begging me to open up to him, begging to taste me, and without a second thought, I open and give him everything he desires at this moment. The taste of honey whiskey awakens my senses and takes me to lengths I didn't think possible. This kiss is needy, demanding, desiring, and comforting. It's fire.

All at once, he's grasping me, my thighs, my hips, my breast.

"I need you, now," he demands with such authority, such conviction in his words.

"Are you sure? I know you never cared for me...."

"Stop, damnit, Harper," pulling my attention with just the flames in his hazel eyes. "I've always wanted you. I just wouldn't let myself go down that road."

"And now?"

"And whatever happens, happens."

Pushing away, "Look, I'm all for one-night stands. Hell, I live for them because I have commitment issues, but you. You're now my roommate. If we go down this road, it will change the dynamic of our relationship. Is that something you want?" I ask, not really wanting to know the answer. I want him so bad, but I know better than this. We have to think about the bigger picture.

"Fuck," he spits out. "You're right. What the fuck are we doing?"

"My thoughts exactly," I lie.

"Harper, I'm sorry. I didn't..."

"Stop apologizing. It takes two. I wanted you as much as you wanted me." And with that confession, he stares me down with those gold-inflicted eyes blazing straight through me. His grasp on my hips tightens, and I feel the burn creep into my pores. Fuck, that gaze alone got my panties fucking wet.

And then, just like that, it's gone.

He releases me, closing his eyes, grabbing his glass, and chugging the rest of his whiskey, giving him the strength to get up and walk away without another word.

Fuck, I've got to get laid one way or another, but for now, Charlie will have to do.

CHAPTER NINE

DOMINIQUE

GODDAMNIT, Harper's right. What the fuck was I thinking? My lust is non-existing compared to the bigger picture, and that's Lucas. I can't believe I was headed down that road again.

Fuck.

Did I not learn from Dayna? Dayna ruined any chance of a woman from SPD to warm my sheets. But did we have fun while it lasted? Fuck yeah. She meant everything to me. Hell, she got me through the bullshit I had to deal with, Keisha. She eased the pain the more we fucked.

A proposition we had.

A condition we needed.

She was getting over her ex, and so was I. We both needed relief and for three years, she was my relief. No one knew other than Ethan, and he wouldn't tell a soul.

When she was killed in the line of duty, it destroyed me. Watching her life slip away before my eyes ripped me apart, and at that moment, I promised never to get attached to another female in the department.

That's why I've been such an ass to Harper. Hell, she never deserved my condescending bullshit, but I had no choice. I had to protect her from me.

Every woman who comes into my life is taken away, and I couldn't do that to Harper. She's too good of a person to destroy.

She's too good for me.

I enter my new room, Harper set up for me. It's fucking nice as shit. With earthy tones of browns, greens, and blues, it gives a serene feel to the place. Something I need right now.

It has a huge walk-in closet and a massive bathroom with state-of-the-art appliances. There's even a private balcony, completely furnished with wicker lounge seating and greenery hanging everywhere.

I chug the rest of the bottle of whiskey, jump into the shower and jack off to the memory of Harper kissing me with those plump lips.

Fuck.

I'm so fucked right now.

I WAKE UP TO MY ASS HITTING THE FLOOR. "SHIT, THAT HURTS." Hell, everything hurts right about now. My head banging, my ass throbbing, and I hear a screeching noise coming from somewhere.

Who the fuck turned on those bright ass lights.

A few moments later, I hear knocking on a door. Then someone walks in. "Dominique, are you okay?" I glance up, my eyes adjusting to the light. I'm pretty sure it's the sun now that I can see. "Oh, I'm so sorry. I —I'll wa—wait until you get dressed," Harper scurries from my room, closing the door behind her.

"Shit, I'm completely naked," looking down at myself. What the fuck happened last night?

I get up off the floor and head into the bathroom and vomit. Puking all my guts out into the toilet. "Shit, I feel fucking horrible."

I pull my ass off the floor, brush my teeth, and wash my face. God, I don't need to do that ever again.

I throw some clothes on and make my way downstairs.

Harper and Lucas are in the backyard in the swimming pool. Lucas living his best life. I haven't seen him this happy in a long time. He needed this move as much as I did.

I make my way to the kitchen, where there is a red drink, a note that says, "Drink Me," and two pills on a small plate.

Thank the heavens for Harper. How the fuck did she know I needed this? Probably because I showed my ass last night. Hell, I don't even remember a thing.

I toss the pills into my mouth and chug the drink down, "Fuck, that's gross. What the fuck did I just drink?"

"My special hangover recipe. I thought you may need it, and from the looks of it this morning, I was right," she tosses at me while coming back into the house.

"I hope I didn't embarrass myself too much, did I?"

"Just say I'm glad one of us was sober enough to make decisions."

"That bad, hun," sitting down at the island. Harper places a plate full of bacon, eggs, and grits. "Man, I can get used to this," I say before I realize.

"Don't get too used to it. We both have to be back to work in two days. Besides, I'm useless, remember?"

Chocking on my bacon, "I—"

"Relax, I'm joking. You didn't call me useless."

"Thank God. I thought I made a complete ass out of myself," I admit.

"Oh, you did. I'm just not spilling the beans," she laughs to herself, and it's like music to my ears. "My little secret."

Lucas' screams pull me from my internal misery, and I glance out the door, "Dad, come on. The water is refreshing."

"Seriously, where does he get these sayings?"

"He's a smart young man. He's going to do great at his new school."

"That he is," I agree. "Coming, buddy. Just have to grab my trunks, and I'll be right out," I yell.

"I'll watch him until you get back."

"Thanks."

"I mean, I've been watching him all day anyway, so why not a few more minutes? You're welcome, by the way," she laces her tone with sarcasm as I make it to the stairs.

"You're right again. My bad. Thank you," taking a bow.

I then exit the room full of regret, not knowing what the fuck I did or said last night. But it seems to not have bothered her in the slightest.

CHAPTER TEN

HARPER

"WHOA," I moan into my pillow, knowing damn well I'm a screamer when it comes to orgasms. My vibrator, Charlie, is nowhere near as good as the real thing, but my gosh, this past week, it has given me life.

All it takes is one vision of Dominique's dick impaling me through the bed, and I lose all concentration. "Jesus Christ," I scream into my pillow.

I've finished playing with Lucas in the pool, and all I can think about is that fucking kiss. The kiss I stopped because my stupid ass was trying to be good for once. "Fuck," I'm almost to my peak when I hear a knock on my door. "Shit! Goddamnit! Fuck!" curse words spewing out like water spilling out of a faucet.

"Coming!" I yell, physically and figuratively.

I clean myself up and then rush to the door, completely out of breath. Opening the door, Dominique stands before me in a pair of jeans hanging off his hips and a white t-shirt hugged around his broad shoulders. Fuck, he looks too damn good. I could fuck him right here, right now, and I wouldn't give two shits what it does to our friendship or living arrangements.

"Yes," I manage to speak through panting breaths.

"Dinner is ready. Would you like to join Lucas and me?" Dominique asks.

"Uh, yes, of course. I'll be right down in just a moment." I go to close the door, but Dominique stops it from shutting, slightly pushing himself through without permission, but fuck it. I need him to take me right now. I'm so goddamn horny.

He glances around and spots Charlie on the bed.

Fuck.

My.

Life.

My cheeks warm to an incredible temperature, and I can't hide it now. I'm so fucking caught right now.

He stares into my eyes, forcing me to see straight through his façade.

I see *need*.

I see *desire*.

I see *lust* and *want* in his gaze.

He wants me as much as I want him, but damnit, does he want me to make the first move or what. I. Will. Not. Stop. Him. This. Time. Because if he touches me right fucking now, I will burst into a million pieces.

I notice conflict in his stance, wanting, no, needing to walk out right now, but his body won't allow him. So, I do the unspoken thing between us, breaking the tension with a slice of my fingernail across his forearm, and that's all the invitation he needs before he lifts me up, slamming the door shut and taking my mouth into his.

I'm not saying a fucking thing to stop this motivated desire. Not one thing.

He's dragging his lips down my neck and around my jawline, tasting, nipping, and sucking me. Finally, he tosses me on the bed, where I bounce slightly from the force. He runs his gaze over my body, and I instantly come into my panties. Good grief.

He lifts my sundress up and rips my panties clean off my body with such force it startles me.

Damnit, those were my favorite.

He slips his shirt over his head, and my God, his body looks like it's been chiseled from the very stone the gods came from.

He bends down, not saying a word because he doesn't have to. It's written all over him what he wants to do to me. He takes my pussy into his mouth, and I fucking lose it. He places his hand over my mouth to muffle my cries while fucking me with his tongue. He's licking every part of my clit, and sucking life into my soul. My hips buck off the bed, and it takes all of his strength to keep me down. Finally, after my extremely powerful orgasm, he stands, taking his pants and boxers off.

And fuck my life, I've never seen such a beautiful dick in my life. He curves a little to the left, and oh my gosh, he has a piercing at the tip, shaped into a dumbbell. He smirks at my internal revelation while climbing on top of me. Such an arrogant ass. But with such a pretty dick, he can be an arrogant ass.

I welcome every inch of his dick and then some. "Oh, God, please," I find myself begging this beautiful creature again for the third time in my life.

"Please, what, Harper," he whispers in my ear, nipping at the cartilage, dripping with seduction and pure lust.

"I need you inside of me, now!" I cry out, "I'm clean and on birth control," I add. I don't give a shit about a condom right now. I want to feel him.

All of him!

Slightly hesitating, "I'm clean too, baby girl," he says while nibbling on my ear. Jesus Christ. "Are you sure?"

"Yes, damnit, I'm sure. Please fuck me—"

And at that very moment, he slams inside me, filling me completely. Finally, I can't get enough and force my hips to buck with his, fucking each other hard and rough, just like I need it, want it, have to have it.

He's pounding into me, giving me all of him, over and over again. "Fuck, baby. You feel so fucking good."

"You like that pussy?" I say, not realizing how dauntless I am in this moment. Dominique brings this side of me out in a way I didn't think possible. But with him, I'm fearless.

"Fuck yeah." He's taken it to a whole new level of intensity when his piercing makes me squirt all over the fucking place. "Fuck, you're a squirter. So, fucking hot," he says between thrusts. My orgasm is so intense my legs and body quiver uncontrollably.

I grip him with my walls as I settle from my high, allowing him the pleasure to fuck me even harder. I needed this so fucking bad I beg for more. And he gives me exactly what I want and need.

I feel him swell inside me, but he pulls out and slams back into me. He reaches underneath me, lifting me off the bed and holding me in his lap while thrusting over and over until I feel myself build again. Never have I ever come more than once. Now, I've come twice and working on my third. Jesus fucking Christ. Dominique is going to be the death of me.

He pulls me closer, like he's trying to fuck straight through me. Grunting with every thrust, he spills every drop of his cum into my now-swollen pussy, emptying himself completely. Finally, we collapse on the bed, intertwined in each other's embrace.

"Fuck, Harper," is all he says after that intense performance.

"I know, right. What the fuck was that?"

"Two years of sex deprivation and that fucking dildo lying on your bed. How dare you deny yourself when I'm right down the fucking hall?" He spits out.

"What?" I question incredulously. "How the fuck should I know that you wanted to fuck me? You haven't exactly been my biggest fan."

"What, last night wasn't proof enough?"

"You remember that?"

"Yeah, it took me a while. But I remember everything. And stop worrying about what might happen. We're grown, adults. We can fuck each other without catching feelings."

"Is that what that was, a simple fuck to take the edge off?" I ask dubiously.

"Wasn't it?"

I get out the fucking bed and put my clothes on. "Yeah." I then walk the fuck out my own room, slamming the door behind me.

Asshole!

CHAPTER ELEVEN

DOMINIQUE

I DONE FUCKED UP...

Again.

I can be a complete ass when I put my mind to it. I haven't seen Harper in three days. Lucas says he sees her every day, but it's clear she's avoiding me at all costs and wants nothing to do with me.

I drop Lucas off at his new school at Godley Station K-8 and head to work. Harper has to see me at work. Right?

I pull up to Northwest Precinct when I receive a phone call from Lieutenant Hall.

"Parker," I answer.

"Hey, Parker. After roll call, meet me in your captain's office."

"Is everything good?" I ask suspiciously.

"Yeah, I just have a few things to go over."

"Okay, I'll be right there after roll call."

Fuck, did Harper report me? Could she be that mad at me? Of course, she wouldn't do that, would she?

We finish roll call, and Harper is nowhere to be found. Sarge said she wanted to extend her leave time, which is within her right. But fuck, I need to speak to her sooner than later.

I enter the captain's office. Captain Sadie, Wilson, and Lieutenant Hall sit at the conference table. I enter apprehensively. What the fuck did I do this time?

"You can close the door," Captain Sadie instructs.

I close the door and stand at attention. "Relax, Parker. You're not in trouble," Captain Wilson admits.

"Yes, sir," I relax a little. But it's not often when you're called to the captain's office, and there are three brasses in the room. "What can I help you with?"

"We need you to join SIU," Lt. Hall states.

"Why?" Did not see that coming. "I'm happy where I am."

"No, you're complacent," Captain Sadie says. "You had so much potential, and when Pierce and Stevens were killed, your fire disappeared. Your desire for this job vanished."

"No, it hasn't; I just don't want to deal with the same shit every day. Excuse my language."

"Oh, we know, but you have something to add to the unit," Lieutenant Hall states.

"And what's that?"

"You remember the City Market shooting, right?"

"Yeah, how could I forget?" I respond sarcastically.

"Well, your ex-wife's new boyfriend, Robert Orangejello Holmes, Jr., has something to do with Pierce and Stevens' shooting." My interest ignites.

"I'm listening."

"We thought you would," Captain Wilson states.

"Orangejello was part of the crew who shot and killed all those in City Market, including Pierce and Stevens. He didn't pull the trigger, but he knows who did. And when your ex-wife stabbed him, he started talking with one of our agents, not knowing he's undercover," Lieutenant Hall states.

"So, what do you want from me and this dude, Orange, something?"

"We need you to reach out to your ex-wife and see if she's willing to work with us."

"Oh, hell no," I blurt out. "That bitch tried to kill me. If I find her, she's fucking dead. And after what they did to my son. Look, man, y'all can't do this to me. I won't. I refuse."

"Okay, okay, we understand. We knew it would be a long shot, but we had to ask," Lieutenant Hall confesses.

"Fuck, y'all got my blood pressure up," I admit.

"Sorry, man. We didn't mean any harm, but if you change your mind. Please let us know. We really need your help, and we know she's the key to getting close to Orangejello," Captain Wilson says.

All I want right now is to speak with Harper to let her know what I said came out wrong, very wrong. I've got to stop fucking around.

"You can go, Parker, but know that we're here if you need us," Captain Sadie ensures.

"Yes, ma'am." I then walk out.

I bump into Ethan and Morris as I exit the captain's office.

"Hey man, what did they want?" Ethan whispers so only Morris and I can hear.

"They wanted me to help with an operation they're having in a couple of days," I answer, scanning the precinct's halls for any signs of Harper. Then, changing the subject, "Hey, have y'all heard from Bradshaw?"

They both look at each other, thoroughly confused. "Aren't you living with her?" Morris asks suspiciously.

"Yeah...I just...uh, never mind."

"No, man, what's up? Something is up. Maybe I can help," Ethan offers, clearly reading through my bullshit.

"I fucked up. Like, seriously fucked up, and she won't speak to me. She's been dodging me all week."

"You fucked her, didn't you?" he seethe underneath his breath so Morris couldn't hear. And when I don't answer, he rips me a new one. "What the fuck, man? What happened to not fucking broads we work with?" throwing air quotes around fucking. "Do you want to go down the same fucking road we went through two years ago?" shoving me into the locker room, away from Morris.

"I know, man. Don't you think I know that?" I spit out in frustration.

"Apparently, fucking not. I was there, man, through it all. You completely lost your shit when Dayna died, discovering that she was gang-raped by those psychos and then left for dead. And when they fucking realized she was alive, they gunned her down like a fucking dog in the street. And then to find out she was pregnant with your kid. It took everything in me to stop you from hunting those assholes down, everything. I can't. I won't see you go through that again."

We then hear something knock over behind us, "Who's there?" I call out in fear; this person just listened to every one of my deepest secrets.

Ethan and I flank both sides of the lockers, walking closer to the last row. Finally, we enter the third row and see none other than Harper.

"What the fuck? I've been trying to call you all day," I rant with more venom in every word than I realized.

"I—I had a few things to get, and besides...hold on," she raises a hand while trying to find the right words. "Ah, yes, we're just fuck buddies, remember. So, what the fuck does it matter to you where the fuck I go," she spits out so harshly I get whiplash just from the words alone. No matter the death stare, she's rockin'.

"I—"

"Fucking save it. I'm a big girl. I can handle blatant disrespect. Oh, and you can continue staying at my house. I'm not a heartless bitch like you, and besides, I would never treat Lucas as bad as you've treated me all these fucking years. He doesn't deserve it, but you, fuck you!" She slams her locker shut and walks past us, leaving our mouths hanging completely open out of pure shock.

"Shit, dude, you really fucked up," Ethan deadpans.

"Fuck, I know. How am I going to fix that?" shoving my hands toward the empty space Harper held only moments ago.

"A lot of groveling and kissing her ass," he replies. "Well, at least she didn't kick your ass out," he laughs out loud. "I told you not to get involved with someone you work with. Now look...you're totally fucked."

"Yeah, tell me about it. Thank God for Lucas."

"You got that right. You owe him and her, big."

"And where to fucking start?"

CHAPTER TWELVE

HARPER

WHAT A FUCKING PRICK. But I can't blame nobody but my damn self. I wanted him; no, I needed him. Fuck, I needed him so bad, and he felt so good inside of me. Not one dude made me squirt in my life, and that right there, bae bae, was fire. He made me feel alive again. Wanted and desired. God, I can still feel the remanence of our intense passion.

But I knew he wasn't ready for no damn relationship. Hell, I ain't either, but it's the principle. Am I not good enough to be wanted or needed? Am I not wifey material?

Serves me right. I should've kept my mouth shut and let that sex God fuck me every night.

Oh well. Now I need to find someone who will...

Those people at the lawyer's office keeps calling me, so I finally gave in. I've decided to cremate my father. I can't fathom watching my father being lowered six feet into the earth. A earth that caused him so much pain. So, now I wear him around my neck, close to my heart in a twenty-four karat gold neckless, encased with diamonds and sapphire stones.

I'm on my way to see them now, and I kinda wish Dominique would come with me, but nope. He needs to apologize to me. Even though I know he's going through a lot right now.

When I overheard Ethan and him talking in the locker room, I was beyond fucking shocked. Yes, it was before my time, but damn. He experienced all that with that officer, um, Dayna Pierce, I think is the name they said. That confession is so heartbreaking. She was carrying his child, and I know how he feels about Lucas, so I can only imagine the devastation he suffered when finding out about his unborn child.

Jesus.

I had to come up with something so they wouldn't think I was eve's dropping on their argument. Hopefully, they don't suspect anything.

I pull into the parking lot of the lawyer's office and head into the building.

"Hi, I'm here to see Mr. West," I explain to the young lady behind the desk. She's very young, maybe a teenager or early twenties. She has such a soft voice, and she's a beautiful, meek young lady.

"Hi. I will let Mr. West know you're here. You can have a seat just over there," she points to the waiting area.

"Thank you." I find a seat and casually look around when I spot some magazines on the coffee table.

I scan through the pile and find one for outdoor spaces. Perfect. I've wanted to work on my home's backyard area and give it a tropical feel. So I flip through the pages and find the ideal setup for my backyard, with the pool and everything. I take a pic of the page, and then I hear my name being called.

"Ms. Bradshaw."

"Yes," I place the magazine back on the coffee table and stand.

"Good Afternoon, I'm West Moore. Everyone calls me West," extending his hand for me to shake.

I take it and give him a nice firm shake, "Hi, I'm Harper."

"Nice to meet you, Harper; my office is right this way." He places his hand on the lower end of my back, making me slightly uncomfortable. Like, why does he need to touch me?

We enter his office, and he closes the door behind me. Now, my spidey senses are up.

"Have a seat while I gather your paperwork." So, you don't have the paperwork already? Like, you knew I was coming.

After a few moments, he returns with a folder. "Here we are." He places the folder in front of him and pulls some documents out. "Okay, yes. Your father, Raymond, left a Will and Trust for you and your future children."

"What Will? He was broke. How does he have a Will?"

"I'm not sure why you think your father was broke. He left you over ninety-five million dollars; some of it is held for any children you may have."

"Yeah, right," I blurt out. "There ain't no way my father had that kind of money. No way. You must have the wrong person."

"Was your mother's name MaryAnn?"

"Yes," I say cautiously. "Why?"

"He made self-explanatory instructions not to leave her anything. He wanted you to have everything, and he left a letter for you in the event he died." Mr. West hands it over, and I take it apprehensively. Like, it's going to combust and burn me alive or something.

"Why? How?"

"He stated everything you needed to know is in the letter," he nods towards my hands, where the letter sits on the tips of my fingers as if it's going burst into ash before my eyes. "Do you have any questions for me?"

"I have a thousand, but I won't overwhelm you. Is there anything else?" I subconsciously twirl my father's pendant between my fingers.

"Yes, ma'am. I just need you to sign these documents to transfer the funds. And I will need a bank account to make the transaction complete. You can leave everything with Miss. Alice up front."

"Is that all?"

"Yes, ma'am. If you have any questions after you read the letter, please don't hesitate to call me."

"Okay."

I fold the letter up and put it in the back pocket of my jeans. I walk out of Mr. West's office, thoroughly confused. All this time, we were millionaires, and my father never said a fucking word.

Was he trying to punish me? Or maybe teach me how to earn my own? But if that's the case, why not tell me about it? I genuinely believe I would still be the independent woman I am today.

I have so many unanswered questions. But I suppose I will find them in this letter.

SITTING ON MY BALCONY, SIPPING ON A GLASS OF RED WINE, holding the infamous letter in my hand, I hear a knock on my door.

"Fuck, what does he want? I just want to be left the fuck alone?"

I hear another knock, so I get up and storm to the door, fire in every fiber of my bones, ready to pounce.

When I snatch open the door with such force, I'm presented with Lucas holding a cupcake in his hand, and my anger shatters and is replaced with delightfulness. This eight-year-old boy has stolen my heart and ran with it. I can't stay mad at all when I'm around such an innocent boy.

"Hi, Ms. Harper. We got you a cupcake from the Grind. They are the best. And Daddy said you were sad, and I didn't want to see you sad, so I got this for you. Do you like it? Please say you like it."

Tears burning the back of my eyelids, threatening to spill over with just a blink, I manage to speak. "Lucas, I love it."

"Yay, I'm so glad, Ms. Harper!" He hands me the cupcake, "It's strawberry. The lady at the Grind said it was your favorite." And I laugh at the sentiment. Dianella surely knows her customers.

"Yes, it is."

"Ms. Harper?"

"Yes?"

"Why are you sad?"

He has no idea how that one little question is such a loaded question. We both sit down against the wall, and I find myself playing with my gold chain.

"Well, I found out something, and I don't know how to process the information."

"What do you mean? What did you find out?"

Not wanting to lie or give this sweet boy too much detail, I contemplate my next words.

"My daddy left me something, and I'm not sure how to accept it."

"My daddy gives me things all the time, and I know he works really hard for them, and he really doesn't have to give me much. But I appreciate it even more because I know my daddy loves me and will always take care of me. So, you should let your daddy take care of you. He loves you, Ms. Harper."

And at that very moment, I break. Like a god-awful break. The words this young soul delivers have me bawling my eyes out.

"Oh, no, Ms. Harper. I didn't mean to make you cry. I'm so sorry, Ms. Harper," Lucas soothing me with his tiny hands.

"No, sweetheart. You didn't make me cry. I—"

"Lucas, son," my head snap up at the thunderous voice. "Let me speak with Ms. Harper. Go to your room and play your game," Dominique instructs his son.

"Is Ms. Harper going to be okay?" Lucas asks with concern in his voice.

"Yes, son, Ms. Harper will be okay."

"Okay, Daddy." Lucas then skips to his room, full of joy.

Lifting me off the floor and pushing me into my room the same way he did last time and closing the door behind us, Dominique urges me to sit on my sofa in my lounging area.

"No, leave me—"

"Harper, stop pushing me away."

"You've done that all by yourself," I spit out. "Just leave me the fuck alone."

"Harper, please let me speak."

"Why the fuck should I?"

"Because damnit?"

"Because what?"

"I care about you, Harper. Is that what you want to hear?"

"I don't want to hear shit from you unless you mean it."

"I do," and with that confession, tears stream down my face heavily. He wraps his strong arms around me, embracing me with such comfort I try to pull away. But of course, he won't let me. "Stop fighting me. Let me care for you like you've cared for me."

This man is breaking me, and I no longer have the strength to fight back. I'm afraid to admit that I need him. Hell, I fucking want him right fucking now. I need him to erase all of the pain, all of the heartache, all of it.

I finally have the strength to push him off me and guide him to the bed, stumbling and fumbling with my jeans and tank top. It finally registers what I want, and he tries to stop me.

"Look, if you're not going to fuck me, then I'll find someone who will. This is what you wanted, right? A fuck buddy?" I bellow.

"Seriously, Harper, that's how you think I see you?"

"Isn't it?"

"Fuck Harper! I can't be the person you want me to be because—"

"I don't want you to be anybody," cutting him off. "I just want to fuck, and if you're not willing, get the fuck out of my room."

He stares at me with such conviction and turmoil. He's fighting within, and I see it written all over his face. But right now, I don't give a shit after what he pulled the other day.

"Fuck it. I'll see you later," I say with such harshness. I begin to put my clothes back on, grab my Michael Kors crossbody and walk out the door. Strong hands wrap around my wrists, pulling me back into the room.

Dominique pushes me onto the bed while completely ripping my shirt off my body. The force gives me life and takes my desire to a whole new level. He yanks my jeans down with such determination it makes my legs weak.

"Is this what you want?" spitting out while taking his clothes off.

"Yes!"

"Fuck, Harper. You have no idea how much you make me fucking insane."

"Then show me," I challenge.

And just like that, Dominique got my pussy wrapped around his tongue, tasting and tugging with such passion and force, yet delicate and demanding. He fucks me senseless with just a tug of my clit and a lick of my inner soul. He brings me to the point of no return, and before I explode, he stops abruptly.

I scream out with the loss of his mouth, "Naw, baby girl. You're not controlling this. I'm the fucking naysayer in this mothafucka," he says with authority in his tone. "Come suck this dick," he demands.

Fuck, he's turning me fucking wild right now, and I can only manage to say in response, "Okay," not ever knowing I had such a submissive side in my life.

I get on my knees and take his ten fucking inches into my mouth. He's so fucking big that I can't manage to get him all the way in without gagging. I wrap my small hands around his shafts while swirling my tongue around his head. I bring him in and out while jacking him off. "Naw, baby girl. No hands; put him all the way in. I want to see you gag on this dick."

I do as he says and force his dick to slide through my gag reflexes. I bob him in and out with such force and carnal need. I bite him a little, and he groans with pleasure. He shoves his hand through my hair and wraps his hand around it, and tugging at my strands, giving me a little boost of energy to make him fucking come.

And then, he snatches me off his dick, picks me up, and drops me on my bed, "I didn't tell you to make me come," he chastises while climbing on top of me. I'm so fucking wet; my juices are sliding down my ass. His aggressiveness gives me life, and I don't know why. "Baby girl, I'm about to be rough with you. Safeword, Alpha. Understand, baby girl?" I don't know why that just made me come all over these sheets, but fuck, I wouldn't care if he fucked me in the ass; I need him now! "Answer me," he demands.

"Yes, I understand, Alpha."

And just like that, he slams his dick inside me, and I scream out in pure ecstasy. He muffles my cries with his kisses while fucking me senseless, slamming in, and then coming back out and thrusting in me so hard.

In this moment, we both needed to feel this. This frustration and aggression are fueling our souls, and I can't get enough. I feel myself build right back up, and this time he lets me squirt all over his dick. I come so fucking hard; I think I peed myself.

"Jesus, baby girl. I need you to fucking do that again," he pants through each thrust, slamming into me over and over again. And just like that, I fucking squirt again, depleting every bit of my energy. "That's it, baby girl. That's my baby girl."

I'm afraid to respond to his sentiment, so I keep my mouth shut, allowing him to feel everything I'm feeling. I need him to understand that I need him now more than ever.

I feel him swell inside, and I know he's on the brink of coming inside me. So I squeeze him as hard as I can with my walls, giving him the momentum to flourish me with his seed.

"Fuck, baby girl. I'm fucking coming. Goddamnit Harper. Fuck!" as he empties inside me, we both collapse in pure exhaustion. I no longer have any fight in me. I just want to go to sleep.

I doze off when I feel Dominique wrap his arms around me, pulling me closer to him.

"Baby girl, I'm truly sorry for how I've treated you, and I will spend the rest of my days making it up to you. I promise you that," kissing me on the back of my head as tears stream down my face once again.

Not saying another word, we both drift off to sleep.

CHAPTER THIRTEEN

DOMINIQUE

HARPER'S BEEN asleep for an entire day, sleeping from complete exhaustion. Who knew she needed to be broke off rough and aggressive. So submissive in the bedroom but nowhere near that outside of it.

She has endured so much, just from what she's told me. And to hear what she told Lucas yesterday broke me down. I had no intention in fucking her yesterday. Just really wanted to comfort her and give her closeness, something we both need right now. Whatever her dad left for her must be huge because I've never seen Harper like this before. Well, to think of it, she does transition into someone completely different when she's working. It's like night and day, oil and vinegar, just the complete opposite of who she is outside of that uniform.

She was devastated and just wanted to feel anything but what she was feeling last night.

Anything.

Lucas comes flying into my room with his Nintendo DS, "Daddy, Daddy. Look, I'm number one! I beat everyone in the world!" he explains enthusiastically. I wouldn't allow him to play so many video games if he wasn't such a genius in school.

"That's cool, buddy. Are you ready to eat?"

"Yes, sir, but can Ms. Harper eat with us? I'm worried about her," his tone changing to compassion. Lucas is just like me when it comes to caring for people; he gives his all.

"Yes, of course. Go wash your hands, and I'll see if she's up to eating something tonight."

"Yes sir," and he takes off like a missile in the sky. I love his energy.

I head to the third floor and knock gently on the door. When I hear a moan, I open it and peek in.

"Hey, baby girl. Lucas and I would like you to join us for dinner if you're up to it."

"What time is it?" she asks groggily.

"It's seven in the evening."

"Huh, what?" Harper jumps out of bed. "I've slept all day?"

"Just about. I didn't want to disturb you. You needed the rest."

"But I have stuff to do before shift tomorrow."

"Baby girl, you've got to stop stressing so much; you'll have a stroke at this rate."

"I work best under stress. Besides, I have to clean, cook, wash clothes…" she trails off while searching for clothes to put on.

"Harper, I've cleaned, cooked, and washed your uniforms. Everything is pressed and hanging on the door frame. I didn't know where you kept your clothes. Everything else is taken care of. We just need your presence at the dinner table. We're having lasagna."

She slows down a tad, but I can tell it's driving her crazy, not having to keep her mind busy.

"Okay, well. Let me get dressed, and I'll be down in a few."

"Okay," closing the door, I head to the kitchen, where Lucas has set the table for three. I grab the lasagna and place it on the pan holders. I pour Harper and myself a glass of McBride Sisters red blend. Black Girl Magic is Harper's favorite brand.

As Lucas and I get everything set up, I give him a high-five, and then he greets Harper at the foot of the stairs.

"Hi, Ms. Harper. Do you feel better?" Lucas asks.

"Yeah, a whole lot better. I think I needed the rest," she answers, glancing at me, knowing she needed more than just sleep. She needed that back broke in, and so did I. I'm getting hard just thinking about it.

Lucas takes Harper's hand and guides her to her seat. "You can sit right here. Daddy and I are sitting on both sides of you because you're the Queen."

And we all burst out laughing. Oh, that laugh is so pure of joy and excitement. To see my two favorite people brings me life. But soon, I'll have to deal with Keisha and that Orange Jell-o dude. Who the hell names their child Orange Jell-o anyways?

Fucking Savannah.

CHAPTER FOURTEEN

HARPER

WEEKS HAVE PASSED, and things are starting to go back to normal. I'm back at work, Dominique hasn't heard from Keisha and her side piece, and Lucas has really adjusted to everything at school and here at my home.

Lucas and I hang out daily, either talking about our days or hanging out by the pool. The construction crew begins their work next week, and I can't wait. Lucas has been instrumental in designing my back-yard to be an oasis and a dedicated play area for when his friends visit. How this little boy has me wrapped around his little fingers is beyond me, but I've certainly gotten attached, whether I wanted to or not.

I don't know how he'll feel about moving soon. Hell, I don't know how I will feel. Dominique and I haven't discussed it. Yeah, our whatever you want to call it has grown into something, but I dare not say a thing. I have no idea where Dominique's mind is, nor do I want to fuck up what we got going on.

He's a fucking God in the bedroom. Taking me to new lengths and breathing breath into my every being. The way he commands me awakened something in me, giving me chills just thinking about it, and

I'll be damned if I make it stop now. If he were to find someone else, I just might have to be his side piece because je-sus, I'm getting wet just thinking about it. Shit.

"Hey, girl, you ready to hit the streets?" Katie asks, bringing me from my own tortured mind.

"Yeah, give me one moment, and I should be ready."

"Okay, I'll meet you at the car."

I was finishing up at the locker when I accidentally knocked an envelope down. Once I bend over to pick it up, I realize it's the letter my daddy left for me. I have yet to read it. The money he left for me is just sitting in the bank. I haven't even touched it or told anyone about it. I pick the letter up and stuff it back into my locker, where I've left it for safekeeping, not that it wouldn't be safe at home. I just. I just don't know.

I exit the locker room and join Katie for our shift. As soon as we get into the unit, we receive a call about homeless people fighting in Johnson Square. Of course, it's a useless endeavor, but whatever, we still ride the call. Once we arrive, Officer Henry and Officer Perez are already engaged with the suspects.

As Katie and I approach, one of the suspects swings an object at Officer Henry, knocking him to the ground. I grab my taser out of the holster and announce, "Taser, taser, taser, stop resisting," giving everyone time to either get out of the way or comply. The suspect tries to hit me with the object; I pull the trigger, hitting him in the chest. He tenses up, falling to the ground, flailing around like a tortured fish. Katie and Perez flip the guy over and handcuff him. I holster my taser after they pull the prongs out of him and then check on Henry. "Are you okay?"

"Yeah. He got me good."

"Here, stay down. Don't try to get up." I get on the radio and ask for EMS and a supervisor. I continue to talk to Henry. "Okay, Henry, I need you to continue to talk with me. You can't fall asleep. We have to make sure you don't have a concussion."

"Did anyone ever tell you that you have pretty eyes?" he asks.

"A time or two, but I don't pay it no mind," smiling at his compliment. I see he hasn't lost his charm.

"You should. Bradshaw, you're a pretty girl. Parker needs to get his shit together before someone else snatches you up. That's what happened to me. I let someone else get Harris because I was too chicken to get her myself."

"What do you mean? Katie isn't with anyone."

"I saw her. They were kissing. I'm so stupid," he slurs.

"You're not stupid. And I'm sure that door is still open. Trust me." And at that moment, Katie walks over to assist me with Henry.

"Oh, Jackson. Are you okay? EMS will be here soon, Katie assures him. "Harper, can you drive the unit? I want to ride with Jackson…to ensure he's okay," Katie explains.

"Sure." I give Henry a wink as I stand and help Perez. That's his chance right there.

As I help Perez with the arrestee, Dominique approaches me. "Hey, y'all alright?"

"Yeah, I had to use force against the arrestee. Where's Sarge?"

"He's in a meeting, so I'm watching out for the unit until he's back."

"Oh, okay. Buddy started swinging that thing and hit Henry in the back of the head. I gave verbal commands for him to stop and called out taser three times. He then swung the object at me, and that's when I tased him. We were able to handcuff him until EMS arrived. I was keeping Henry awake, but Katie took over. She's going to ride with him to the hospital."

"Are you sure you're okay?" he whispers to me.

"Yeah, I'm sure. He didn't hit me."

"Okay. Great work. I'll let Sarge know."

I walk away when Dominique grabs me by the wrist, bringing me closer to him. I feel the pull between us instantly. The carnal need.

"Yeah," is all I can manage to say under his heavy seductive gaze.

"I need to speak with you after work."

"Okay," and before he let go, he brushes his lips against my ear, and I nearly come all in my panties. "Shit, you can't do that at work. Someone may see us."

"Well, you shouldn't look so damn good in that uniform."

"Tonight. We'll talk tonight."

"That's all I ask."

He then let me go, and man, I feel all giddy inside.

KATIE ENDED UP STAYING WITH HENRY, WHICH I ALREADY expected her to. So, therefore, I ended up riding calls with Perez. He's not a bad guy to partner up with; he just doesn't know my quirks.

We received our last call for today, which is in Parker's and Ethan's beat. But they're on a domestic call right now.

The call is in reference to a woman with a gun, pacing back and forth like she's in distress. There's no other description, but we have multiple calls coming in.

"Alright, you ready?" I ask Perez.

"We got this," he answers.

"Okay, I'll approach the female to bring the focus to me," I instruct.

"Okay, that's fine with me."

A few minutes later, we arrived on the scene. We exited the vehicle immediately, running directly into the distressed female. She has the gun pointed at us and pulls the trigger.

"Fuck, Perez, get down," I yell and then ask for backup ten-eighteen. "Metro, shots fired, shots fired! We need backup now!" I announce on the radio.

While returning fire, I realize Perez is nowhere to be found. Three of my shots hit the woman, causing her to collapse to the ground. As I get ready to search for Perez, I'm stuck with something in my neck.

"Ouch," I turn around and pull the trigger, hitting my attacker. But, as I plunge to the ground, I realize there is more than one person. Closing my eyes, I see Perez on the asphalt suffering from a gunshot wound to the neck, his hands wrapped around the wound, trying to stop the bleeding. "No!"

CHAPTER FIFTEEN

DOMINIQUE

ETHAN and I flying to assist Harper and Perez. We're doing at least a hundred to get there. "God, this can't be happening again. Not again," I cry out.

"Parker, calm down. We don't know anything yet."

"Fucking hurry up then."

"All units, all units, officers are down. Officers are down. We're now patching all channels," the dispatcher announces after the alert tones ring out. "We have one officer still at the scene; the other has been taken.

"Fuck!!!!" I spit out.

"All units, the officer was last seen dragged into a black dodge challenger with Georgia plates. The officer is Bradshaw."

"Fuck!"

Before Ethan can put the fucking car into park, I jump out and dash straight to the scene. Officers and EMS already have Perez in the ambulance and heading to the hospital.

What the fuck is going on. That's three officers in one fucking day. Ethan then calls my name. I spin around to see what he wants.

"Man, it's Keisha. Keisha is the one that was shot."

"Wha—"

"Man, I'm sorry."

"No, it can't be. Where the fuck is Harper?"

"According to the witnesses, Keisha was pacing back and forth with a gun. When Perez and Bradshaw arrived on the scene, Keisha started shooting at them immediately. They had no chance to react any other way than this outcome. She hit Perez in the neck, but Bradshaw was able to get behind the car and shot Keisha three times. But Keisha wasn't alone. Three others pulled up behind Bradshaw. She was able to shoot and kill one, but the other two grabbed her and threw her into the challenger. The witness said it looked like they drugged her with something."

"Fuck!"

"Parker, I'll call the Lieutenant and Captain. Check the flock cameras to see if the car has been spotted by one of them."

As soon as he said that, the dispatcher announced, "All units, the vehicle has been spotted going east on Bay Street heading towards the islands. This information has been shared with Thunderbolt and Tybee Island PD."

I jump into my unit, leaving Ethan to sort the shit at the scene.

Not again…not a fucking again.

CHAPTER SIXTEEN

HARPER

WAKING UP IN AN UNFAMILIAR PLACE, I feel groggy and dehydrated. It's a little dark, but I can still see. There are no windows, but light is seeping underneath the door.

All my clothes have been taken off me, including my bulletproof vest, duty belt, and shoes.

"What the fuck? What time is it? How long have I been here? How in the world did I get myself into this shit. I'm so fucked right now."

I hear voices above me, and it heightens my alertness. I've got to get the fuck out of here. Now.

I can't determine what they're saying, but they are definitely men.

I hear footsteps, which is my moment, fight or flight. But if anyone knows me, it's about to go down. Ain't gonna sit around and let these assholes rape me without a fight. Best believe that!

And then the door clicks.

CHAPTER SEVENTEEN

DOMINIQUE

TWO YEARS AGO, BEFORE THE CITY MARKET SHOOTING

"DOM, *please, I can't do this anymore. Either we're in a relationship, or we're done. This thing between us is not working for me,"* Dayna waved her fingers between us.

"Dayna, baby, I don't know if I can. Keisha is still fucking with me, and I don't want to start something with you, and I haven't closed that door. You know how she is," I try my best to explain to her. But, Lord knows I don't want to lose her, but I can't give her what she wants. Not now.

"But you simply have started something with me," putting her hand up to stop me from responding. "I know, and that's why it's time for me to go. I have to find myself. I can't do that here. Watching you with her is killing me," she cries. And at this moment, I want to comfort her, but I know I must let her go. "I'm giving Sarge my two-week notice. I'm going back home."

"Can I see you one last time?" I place my palm on her delicate cheek, stroking it with my thumb.

Caving into my touch, "Yes, one last time, and then we're done." We stand in each other's embrace momentarily when Dayna pulls away. "I have to head to City Market for crowd control. Hell, we both do."

"Yeah, I know. I just... never mind."

She looks at me with such conviction, such emotion. Her skin glowing in the moonlight, radiating through my very being. God, I want her so bad, but she's right. I keep dragging her along. I have to deal with Keisha and her foolishness before I can give her my entire heart.

PRESENT DAY

Deja Vu is a fucking bitch. But, no, not deja vu. This is my fucking reality. Everything that I touch fucking dies on me or gets seriously hurt.

"Fuck!" I yell out to no one in particular. I'm in this fucking car by myself, not a fucking clue as to where I'm going.

Fucking Keisha, yet again, fucked my life. How can she hate me so much? Even in death, she's still fucking with me. I did nothing to that crazy bitch. But she got what was coming to her. It was only a matter of time. Those thugs drugged her, fucked her, and used her to get what they wanted. Now, look at her, dead in the middle of the fucking streets.

The fucking irony of it all. Harper killing my pain in my ass. Go figure.

Slamming my fist on the fucking steering wheel, I'm so fucking furious. I decide to call the babysitter to make sure Lucas is okay.

"Hi, Mr. Parker," Rachel answers after a couple of rings.

"Hi, Rachel. I'm calling to check on Lucas. Can you put eyes on him right now?"

"Sure. Is everything okay?"

"Not really, but it will be soon." She knows my job can sometimes be a little scary, so she never asks for specifics.

"Lucas is in his room playing video games. Would you like to speak with him?"

"Yes, please, if you don't mind."

"Mr. Parker, he's your son. Of course, I don't mind."

She then hands the phone to Lucas, "Hey, buddy."

"Hi, dad. How's work? How's Ms. Harper? Did y'all arrest any bad guys?" and just like that, it takes everything in me not to fucking break.

Taking a deep breath, trying to compose myself as much as possible for my very impressionable son, "We're fine. Just checking on you."

"Okay, dad. Love you."

"Love you too, son."

"And dad?"

"Yeah?"

"Watch over Ms. Harper. She needs us."

"Sure, thing, son."

He then hangs up, and everything I had built up inside of me comes crashing through the imaginary wall.

"All units, stand by for a bolo. All units, be on the lookout for a black Chevy Challenger, possibly in the area of West St in West Savannah. Last seen parked behind a known drug house. Use caution, at fifteen hundred hours," dispatch announces.

That's right up the street from the precinct. So they didn't head to the island after all.

CHAPTER EIGHTEEN

HARPER

MY HEART IS SLAMMING into my chest, adrenaline washing over me. Then, as the door opens, without another thought, I charge, knocking the first guy to his knees.

Another points his gun and shoots at me, but I move out of the way, slamming my fist into his jaw.

He barks out in pain, "Fuck! You bitch!" He tries to recover, but I've already disarmed him, taking the gun and shooting both in the back of the head.

I exit the room and head down a hallway with three closed and locked doors. I then continue down the hall when I hear voices coming from outside.

"Shit, there's more men." I scan the room for anything I can use, but the space is totally bare. "Fuck."

I head back toward the room I was in. I drag the bodies further into the room and set them against the wall. I take the other gun from the holster and sit and wait for the next set of guys.

I'm not sure how much time passes before I hear heavy footsteps in the hall, at least three distinctive step patterns.

I set one of the bodies in front of me to shield my body; if they get a chance to shoot back, I need them to hit these pricks, not me.

I hear the doorknob turn. Allowing two to enter, I shoot two rounds, hitting both in the chest. The third and the fourth enters, shooting AK-47s, I feel my skin get punctured with at least four of the rounds, maybe five or six, but I don't feel pain. I feel the skin break and the warm liquid spill, but no pain.

I pull the trigger until the magazine is empty. Then, the gunfire ceases, and I think I've eliminated my threat.

I start to feel pain in my stomach, shoulder, and legs. I look down, and I have wounds in both my legs, left arm, and three to my stomach. I must stop the bleeding to survive this, but I have no clothes or anything to create a tourniquet.

I feel around for the guys' belts to use. Then, once I get the straps, I wrap them around my legs and arm, screaming out in pain as I tighten them.

Taking a deep breath, I try my best to pull one of their shirts off to put pressure on my stomach. I feel myself getting weak, but I have to hold on to stay alive for any type of help.

Then I remember that they may have phones.

I search one of their pockets and find a phone. Unfortunately, it's locked, but I can still call 9-1-1. So I push the emergency number.

"911, what is your emergency?"

"Bradshaw, payroll 113344. I've been shot multiple times and losing consciousness very soon. I have no idea where I am. Triangulate the cell phone to find me," I spit out quickly, blood dripping from my lips. I know it's only a matter of time before I pass out.

"Oh, God, Bradshaw. This is April. We have everyone looking for you. I need you to continue talking to me. Did you triage your wounds?" April asks with so much concern in her voice.

"Yes," I respond very meekly.

"I have to keep you talking."

"Okay," I feel myself drifting. "April."

"Yes, sweetie?"

"Please tell Dominique...." and then I feel myself drift slowly. April's voice disappearing into the atmosphere.

"Bradshaw. Please stay with me. Harper, please stay with me. The units are almost there. Just hold on a little while longer."

"I love you, Dom—"

CHAPTER NINETEEN

DOMINIQUE

"DISPATCH, I'M ON SCENE," I yell into the radio. Dispatch had Harper on the phone. She was on the fucking phone!

I'm running to the address at full speed. Typically, there are people everywhere, selling dope, drinking at the shot houses, and just being a nuance to society, but not today; there's a first for everything. Makes you wonder why it's so eerie.

The hood knows what's up...

The home is boarded up, the grass overgrown, and derelict vehicles on the side of the house. There is a black challenger in the lane of the home and two blacked-out SUVs in front of the home.

I kick in the door without announcing myself or having a warrant in hand. At this point, I don't give a shit. I have my duty weapon drawn and scan the room for any signs of life.

I make it to the hallway, where I see three deceased bodies in a room's doorway. I head in that direction and find three more bodies but wait. I see Harper, and she appears to be...

"No, please, no."

I drop to my knees and pray to God she's not dead. I check for a pulse and thank the heavens she has one. Yes, it's faint, but there's one.

I hear Ethan announce himself at the front of the house.

"I'm back here. Call for an ambulance. She's still alive."

"It's going to take EMS a minute to get here. We have to take her ourselves."

"Fuck, not again. She cannot die on me. Not again."

"Parker, we got this. Grab her arms, and I'll grab her feet."

I do as he says and walk through the abandoned house and then place her in the back of the patrol car. I then get in with her, and Ethan drives. I put as much pressure on her wounds on her stomach. It looks like she stopped the bleeding in her legs and arm.

"Fuck, she did all of this all by herself," I say, not really to anyone in particular.

"She's a tough one. You know that. When you gonna take your head out of your ass and tell her how you truly feel."

"What do you mean?"

"Man, I can see it written all over you. You love Bradshaw. You're different with her than Dayna and Keisha."

"How so?"

"Keisha was something you were afraid to let go of because she had always been there through high school and college, and then when Lucas came, it was more of an obligation. Then with Dayna, I think you were afraid of losing that feeling she gave you. She made you forget Keisha, and once it was gone, it destroyed you. But with Bradshaw, I see how you look at her and care for her. It's different, man. And Lucas, that kid, is obsessed with her. He loves her wholeheartedly, and she feels the same way about him. Finding a woman who loves you and your kids is hard. She's a keeper. You're afraid of losing her too, and you must stop being afraid. Every circumstance is different."

I hear every word he spills, and still, I have reservations. Bradshaw is literally dying in my arms. I can't think about that other shit right now. I have to make sure she's okay.

We pull up to the Emergency Room, and the staff takes over from there.

Deja fucking Vu...

HOURS HAVE PASSED, AND STILL, NOTHING. NOT ONE WORD from the doctors. It's driving me insane.

It seems like the entire department is here to include Harris and Henry. Henry was injured earlier but was released a couple of hours ago. Harris stayed by his side the whole time, and now I see them holding hands. Perez is still in surgery.

A nurse approaches us, and we all get eerily quiet.

"Hi, I'm Nurse Jamie. By any chance, is Ms. Bradshaw's family here?" she asks as her eyes scan the crowd.

"No, well, her father died a couple of months ago, and her mother, well, she's nowhere to be found. So we're her family," I confess with all my heart. She's my family.

"Well, we can't give you all the details, but she'll be in the ICU for a while. You can visit only two at a time."

"We'll take that! Harris, would you like to see her first? I know she would want you by her side."

"Actually, you're the person she wants to see when she wakes up. Trust me." And with that, I stand and allow Nurse Jamie to guide me to the back.

"I know you can't go into details, but will she be okay?"

"It's hard to say, but we do know if it weren't for y'all taking care of her wounds in the field, it would've been a different outcome."

"Oh, no. She did that all by herself. She created the tourniquet and put pressure on her stomach once I arrived. She saved herself. I did nothing."

"You got her here. That counts, too," she assures me. "Look, I shouldn't say anything, but after hearing the other officer, I feel you two are more connected than you want to admit."

"Okay," stopping shortly after to give her my undivided attention.

"She had six gunshot wounds. None of them exited, so we had to surgically remove each bullet. We were concerned about her reproductive organs the most. If we didn't complete a hysterectomy, she would have died."

"What are you saying?"

"She will never be able to have children the natural way. However, if she chooses to go that route, we did save some of her eggs for surrogate purposes."

"My God. This will crush her," shoving my hands through my disheveled curls.

"Yes, we know. That's why it's important for her to be surrounded by loved ones. She's going to need the support."

"Okay. I will make sure it happens. We're roommates, so I'll take time off work to ensure she gets what she needs."

"I'll leave you two for a bit of privacy."

"Thanks, Nurse Jamie."

As she leaves the room, closing the door, I'm surrounded by beeping sounds from the machines. Harper, God, she's so peaceful at this moment, feeling no pain or facing any heartache. I was so worried she would end up like Dayna but thank goodness her fate is so different.

Ethan was right. I have to have faith she will pull through.

I will have faith.

CHAPTER TWENTY

DOMINIQUE

TWO WEEKS AFTER THE CITY MARKET SHOOTING TWO YEARS AGO

ICE-COLD WATER SPLASHING *on my body, waking me from my stupor instantly.*

"Ah, fuck!" I groan.

"Get the fuck up, man. You've been in this house for two weeks now. No one's heard from you or seen you," Ethan barks. "And go put on some damn clothes!"

"Fuck you!" I spit out. "I'm in my own fucking house."

"Yeah, and what about Lucas? Hun, what will he think with his dad pissy drunk and passed out?"

"Fuck you!" I spit out again.

"No, fuck you for making me do this shit!" he yells back. "I know you loved her, but you have to let her go. She's gone, man, and there's nothing either of us can do about it. Nothing."

"I should've been there. I could've protected her," I cry out.

"We had to respond to a call. Yes, it was a bullshit call, but that's the job. Sometimes we have to respond to bullshit calls, and sometimes we respond to more serious calls. We can't be everywhere. We just can't."

"But, why her? Why not me or you or anyone else?"

"Look, dude, I'm the first to know exactly what you're going through. I was there with you, but there was no way of knowing those assholes would kill all those people. We had no idea."

My head's banging with excruciating pain, and my heart racing like it's about to explode at any moment. Fuck this shit.

I jump to my feet, but of course, that was a bad fucking idea. Jesus.

"Here, sit down and drink this," Ethan handing me a glass of red and green shit. "It tastes like shit, but trust me, it will help."

I throw the contents back, chugging every bit of this disgusting shit he's given me. "Fuck, that's gross," I groan.

"Serves you right. Now that I have your attention, I have something to tell you. And yeah, you're not going to like it."

"Fuck, what the fuck else could it be?" I question.

"Dayna was pregnant."

My head snapped up, "She what?"

"Yeah, dude, she was pregnant. Like eight weeks. I doubt that she knew."

"How the fuck do you know this?"

"They did an autopsy, remember. With In-line deaths, we always have to perform an autopsy."

"Fuck," and at this very moment, I bellow over, vomiting everything back up and pissing myself, for fucks sake. "No, she can't... she wasn't... she, how?"

"How the fuck do you think?"

"I—was I her only partner?"

"Seriously, dude, are you calling her a whore now?"

"Fuck, no, no, I'm not, but—oh, God, she was raped," I spit out with dread spilling from every syllable.

"She was raped two weeks prior to her death. She couldn't be pregnant from that. However, I believe she was already pregnant, and the docs didn't catch it the first time she was in the hospital."

"Oh, my, God..."

"Yeah, the baby was yours, bro."

Falling back down, slipping on my own vomit, everything just comes crashing down on top of me. Every blow to the gut, every hit to the head, every slap to the face comes crashing down on me.

Fuck my life!

CHAPTER TWENTY-ONE

HARPER

SIXTEEN YEARS EARLIER

OH, *I can't wait to see mommy and daddy today. I have so much to tell them about the first day of school. I have a new best friend, Jamie. And my teacher is really nice. She let us play outside, sing songs, and paint. I learned new numbers and already know my A-B-Cs, just like daddy taught me.*

Ms. Smith was so proud of me. She made me the class leader. She's the best ever.

My bus pulls to the end of the street. "That's strange. Daddy said he would be here to wait for me," I frown a little, searching out the window as the bus comes to a stop. Girls at six years old aren't allowed to walk by themselves.

"Harper, do you see your parents?" the nice bus driver asks.

"No, ma'am. My daddy said he would be here," I pout meekly, searching the crowd of parents waiting for their kids. My daddy forgot. He never forgets.

"I can walk her home. We live next door," my neighbor, Ms. Jessica, offers. Her daughter and son are older than me. They're twins and are in the eighth grade.

"Are you sure? I can't leave without an adult being here," the bus driver says.

"Yes, of course. I'm sure they're just running a little late," Ms. Jessica explains.

I take Ms. Jessica's hand, and she helps me down the stairs. I then start walking with Sophie and Sam. "Hi Sophie, hi Sam," I wave to both of them. They sit in the back of the bus with all the older cool kids.

"Hey, Harper. How was your first day of school?" Sophie asks.

"It. Was. Amazing," I emphasize with my arms.

"Wow, that's great. Ms. Smith is pretty cool. I had her for my first year as well."

And then, all of a sudden, the mood changes, and Sophie steps in front of me, shielding me from something. What is that? I hear screaming.

Wait....

Is that mommy yelling?

"I can't do this anymore. You're smothering me! You both are!" she yells at the top of her lungs.

What does smothering me? Pulling on Sophie's arm, "What does that mean? Smothering?"

"Uh—."

"Please, honey, come inside. Let's talk about this. Harper needs you. I need you," my daddy begs. I see tears run down his face with red-stricken eyes, pleading, begging.

Mommy snatches out of his grasp, almost knocking daddy down, and runs to the car, throwing all her stuff in the car. She doesn't even look my *way. She then jumps in the car and drives off, and little do I know, my life changed forever at that very moment.*

Crying, Sophie and Sam guide me into their home while Ms. Jessica talks to daddy.

"Why is mommy so mad? What does that word mean? I need my dictionary," shuffling through my backpack. "Is daddy okay? Do you know what's going on?" I ramble the questions out continuously.

"Harper, I'm not sure what's going on, but my mom will make sure everything is okay. Then we will walk you over. Right Sam?" she asks him.

"Uh, yeah. Right. We'll take you home," he answers with a bit of worry in his tone. "Everything will be okay!"

PRESENT DAY

My eyes flutter open slowly, adjusting to the light, panicking slightly; not knowing where I am. I try to remember something, anything, but everything is so fuzzy. Finally, once my eyes get acclimated to the light, I glance around to figure out where I am.

White walls surround me, I hear beeping sounds, and I realize I can't speak. There's a tube or something in my throat. Strong hands wrap around my fingers when I try to pull it out, halting me. I peer over my eyelashes and see a beautiful, no, an inconceivably captivating specimen, skin so pure, I want to lick his face. His robust features are so attractive, yet worrisome, yet still, I want to drink every bit of his creamy milk chocolate up. I imagine my fingers running through his curly dark brown hair and wonder if he's all mine? Do I know this fine creature?

Why on earth am I thinking of sex at a time like this?

While placing my hands by my side, 'cause face it, I have no desire or strength to stop him from touching me. He feels so good. "Harper, baby girl. You can't pull the breathing tube out yet. The doc will be right in."

Baby girl? Is that his pet name for me? Could this fine man really be mine?

Down, girl, you can't get all worked up. Not now, anyway.

"Are you feeling any pain?"

I shake my head no.

"Okay."

He takes my hand in his, and I allow it. Just his calloused touch alone gives me unbelievable comfort. Something I didn't think I needed but definitely desired it. I have no idea why I'm feigning for this strange man, but my God, I pray it never stops.

The feeling, that is.

The doctor, I assume, strolls into the room, and he's just as fine as this guy standing next to me. All of this testosterone got me hot and bothered.

What the fuck is wrong with me?

"Hi, Harper. I'm Doctor Gene Oliver, but you can certainly call me Gene," he greets me with such an infectious smile, shaking the guy's hand standing on the other side of my bed.

"Harper, are you ready to get that tube taken out?"

I nod my head vigorously. So ready.

He instructs me to take a deep breath and then exhale completely while he pulls the tube out. It's more like a colossal cough, but whatever. I'm just glad it's out.

The cute guy hands me a cup of water to soothe my coughing fits, but I know all too well not to drink too much. My daddy… hold on, where is my daddy? Why isn't he here?

My throat is a little sore, but I try to speak anyways.

"Hi, Doctor Gene. Where's my dad? Is he here?" The cute guy and the doc exchange a look, and I know there's something wrong. "What? What's wrong?"

"Harper, do you remember why you're here?" Dr. Gene asks.

"Um, I'm not really sure. I—I don't remember," panic rising deep inside, "Wait…Why? What happened? Why can't I remember?" bile rising in my throat.

Ignoring the question, "What do you remember?" Dr. Gene asks.

"Um, okay, yes. I'm in the academy," relief swirling. "My dad can't be here. He's in the rehab facility. Did I injure myself during training? Is that why I'm here?" glancing between the doc and the cute guy. "Are you from the department?" I ask the cute guy.

"Well, yes, I am from the department, but—"

Cutting the cute guy off, "Um, Harper, what day is it?" Dr. Gene asks.

Glancing back to Dr. Gene, "It's April thirteenth."

"What year?"

"Twenty-nineteen. Why?"

"Because its twenty twenty-two. And I think you're suffering from amnesia," overwhelming dread seeping into my bones as the doctor speaks, clogs my hearing and breathing. I'm—I'm—hot. I'm so hot. "Harper, there's no reason to be alarmed now. Most people get their memory back within a couple of weeks. Traumatic events caused a little memory loss, but nothing too extreme. Your other motor functions are working well, and I believe you will recover very soon," Dr. Gene explains as the cute guy soothes my arm with his caresses. Something I didn't know he was even doing. The touch is actually calming me.

"So, what did happen?" I ask apprehensively.

"Well—"

"Let me tell her, doc," the cute guy interjects.

"Okay," urging the cute guy to speak.

"Hold on, what's your name?" I ask the cute guy.

"My name is Dominique. Dominique Parker. I'm your roommate," he states calmly, but fearfully. I watch him closely. His dimples pulsating, his jaw ticking, and his teeth slightly grinding.

"Oh, I see. But, wait, I live with my father," I interject.

"I'll explain everything in just a moment. But let me get through what happened to you first. If that's okay."

"Okay," closing my mouth and urging myself to keep quiet.

"You responded to a call where you and your partner, well, temporary partner, had to return fire on an active shooter. You shot and killed the shooter; however, she wasn't alone. You were ambushed and taken during the incident. As you were trying to escape, you were shot six times. You performed life-saving measures to keep yourself alive until we could get to you. You were then transported here, where the doc stepped in," Dominique explains. Pretty sure it's more to this story, and this is the chicken-noodle soup water-downed version.

"Yes, we performed, all together, six surgeries over the course of seven weeks," I slightly gasp at, I'm not really sure...the surgeries performed to keep me alive or being in this place for seven weeks and nowhere near aware of any of this. "Don't be too alarmed," that word again, shaking my head. "It's normal to have that many when you've suffered as much as you did. My team is the best in this area. We weren't going to let anything happen to you while you were on my table," the doc reassures me. "Harper, it's going to be a long road ahead, but I believe you will recover beautifully," pausing a moment.

"What?" I sigh, the silence becoming deifying at this point.

"There's more," Dr. Gene states.

"What more can there be?" I question incredulously.

"Well, during the surgery, we had to conduct a Hysterectomy, removing your entire uterus, including your cervix," Dr. Gene explains. "When you were shot in the abdomen, it caused a lot of damage."

"Um, okay...I see. So...what does this mean for me? What are you saying?"

"Harper, you can no longer have children the natural way. I did save some of your eggs if you would like to go the surrogate way, which many women have successfully done." When I don't respond to this devastating revaluation, "Harper?"

I look up at the mention of my name, but I'm unsure how to respond to this information. Like, what does he want me to say?

"You have options," he continues when I don't speak. "That's what matters. Building a family and a life with children is not x'ed out completely," Dr. Gene assures me.

"I just can't give birth...."

Well, I'm glad one of us is optimistic. Because right now, I think I'm about to lose my shit.

"And I'll be there along the way to help with everything. I won't leave your side, well, if that's okay with you, that is?" Dominique offers.

"Yes, if you're my roommate, I'll definitely need your assistance. But unfortunately, I have not a clue as to what to react to or how to react at this moment. I'm—I'm so overwhelmed with so much information right now."

"It will certainly be that way for a while until you're able to get your bearings," Dr. Gene states.

"I know. I just—I don't know. You're basically telling me that I've lost three years of my life, and I may or may not get it back. I can't ever have children, and to be honest, I don't think I ever thought about having kids now anyways. But, in the future, maybe. I'm so confused... literally an understatement. I just don't know. I need to speak to my father. Please call him. I need him. I know he's in the facility, but maybe since I'm a cop, or are you a cop too, Dominique?"

"Yeah, I'm a cop, but I won't be able to help you contact your father."

"Why not?" I yell in frustration, a little too loudly. I didn't mean to be so rude. I'm just so—ugh!

"Because your father died two months ago," he deadpans.

And just like that, I fucking lose it in front of this stranger...

Fuck. My. Life. Damnit, I hate this!

How the fuck did I get to this pitiful level?

How?

CHAPTER TWENTY-TWO

DOMINIQUE

IT'S LIKE AN OUTER-BODY EXPERIENCE, just knowing Harper is okay, but then, she not knowing who the hell I am.

Damnit, man, what the fuck am I supposed to do with that? On the one hand, she can't remember the bullshit I put her in, and we can certainly start from scratch; on the other hand, she doesn't remember the amazing sex we had, not once, but twice, the bone-chilling connection we have.

I've never felt anything like it, not even with Dayna. I don't know how to describe it. I ain't never been into my feelings type of shit. I guess Ethan was right. Damn him.

The torturous moments of just waiting, hoping, and dreaming of the second Harper came to me were monumental for me, to say the least. After Dayna, no, after Keisha, I just didn't give a fuck. I had that 'fuck them hoes' mentality. But, with Harper, it's different.

Of course, the doctor wants to keep her for a few days. Why wouldn't he? Having to tell her her father had passed away was unbelievably difficult. That's one thing I didn't want to explain to her after realizing she had no recollection of who I was. Hell, she thought I was one of the recruiters for the department. Damn, she won't remember anyone from Alpha watch, not even her partner and best friend, Katie.

And now I'll be forced to tell her the whole truth, and let's not forget she can never have children again...she was devastated by the news of her father, and now, she will never be able to continue her bloodline, fuck. Well, in the traditional way, anyways.

Damn, how will she react to my having a kid? She made it very clear she never even thought about having children. Does she want kids? Does she hate kids? Fuck, we never talked about it. She seemed to take a good liking to Lucas. There's no way she hates kids. No way!

I open the front door to Harper's home, hoping to see my beaming son. He always brightens my day after a tragic moment.

He's been hanging out with Ethan for the past several weeks, with me checking in every once in a while. He was so thrilled to hang out with Uncle Ethan that he didn't notice my mood change or the devastation in my voice.

Truth is, I'm in love with Harper, and now I don't ever think I can cross that line ever again, and it's pissing me off. I fucking hate the shit we've had to endure.

Doc told me to get Harper a journal to jot things down in hopes of recovering her memory, but I'm not very optimistic. All I know is I have an open slate now. I can start completely over with Harper now that she doesn't remember the cruelty I put her through.

It's time to get my shit together and win her back.

CHAPTER TWENTY-THREE

HARPER

UGH, I'm so ready to break out of this joint. I'll sell my soul if I can leave now. I already told these people I don't remember anything. So just let me go, and I promise I won't be back.

Dominique called and said he would be taking me home. He's been such a godsend. I don't know what I would've done without him.

Several others came to my room with cards, gifts, and flowers, and I had no clue who these people were. But they've been great with not asking so many questions.

Dominique must've heaved a warning. Thank goodness for that man.

I hear a knock on the door as I put on some black tights, a white tank top, and an oversized sweater.

"Come in," I announce as I put my hair in a messy bun. A task, to say the least, but I pride myself in being self-sufficient.

As I turn to welcome the person entering my hospital room, my breath hitches in my throat. My cheeks blaze with a tinge of warmth, and I find my nipples hardening under the thin cotton.

Oh, God!

"Hey, Harper, are you ready?" Dominique asks in such a seductive way I nearly come in my panties. Jesus, I've got to get my shit together, but hot damn. He's fine!

He's wearing a pair of faded jeans, a hoodie with the saying 'God is Dope' and a pair of all white air forces.

Clearing my throat, "Um, yes. Just gathering a few things that people left for me."

"Here, let me help."

"Thanks," I say over my shoulder. "I didn't realize I had such a fan club."

"Yeah, there are people who love and adore you. Not just because you're a cop, but because you're a beautiful soul, inside and out."

And, of course, I blush at the sentiment, "Thank you for saying that."

We grab all the flowers, bears, and cards and head out of the room. I turn back, a little hesitant to leave, a little worried I'll fail.

I got this.

Harper, you can do this, like anything else in your life...you can also defeat this setback.

We step outside, and I'm greeted with cool air, wishing I wore something slightly thicker, but whatever; it's only a short distance from the exit to Dominique's GMC Denali edition white truck. Well, guessing it's his truck.

I have so much to ask him.

Once Dominique loads all my stuff in the bed of the truck, he helps me climb into the passenger seat. I still have a little trouble with my strength, but the doc says it will improve with time and physical therapy.

As we drive away and emerge onto the highway, I notice we're not heading to my apartment. "Hey, where are we going? My apartment is on the Southside."

"Sorry, I keep forgetting...you purchased a home in the Highlands area. You built it for you and your dad before...well, before he passed. Your goal was to have your own space, and your dad has his, and still take care of him."

"Oh, I see. I wonder if it's the home I designed myself," thinking out loud.

"Actually, it is. You worked every moment of the day, saving every penny to finally get your dream home."

"Well, if it's my dream home, I can see why I asked you to stay with me. It would've been very lonely to stay alone in such a lavish home."

"Also, I have something else to tell you," he spills with concern or fear, or hesitation in his tone. Not sure which.

"Okay," urging him to continue, no fear necessary.

"My eight-year-old son, Lucas, lives with us as well."

"Oh, I see," not really sure how to respond to that confession. I didn't realize he had a kid, but if he's staying with me, I must've been cool with it. Right?

"There's so much I need to explain, but the doc said that I have to allow you to figure things out on your own... but I'm torn with what information to reveal and which to allow to come back to you, naturally."

"No, it's okay. I get it. It's very frustrating not being able to think for myself; having to depend on anyone for anything is not me at all. I just want my life back."

"You will."

"So, tell me about Lucas," changing the subject, but really wanting to know more about this mysterious creature.

"Oh, boy. That little man brought so much joy into my life. He's changed me completely, and I wouldn't alter not one thing about him. To say he saved me is an understatement."

He hands me a phone that shows pictures of a joyful boy, full of life and excitement.

"He's a handsome young boy...just like his daddy...uh, I meant...um—"

"Harper, I know what you meant," chuckling to himself.

Ugh, I'm such an idiot. I know how to handle myself around men. Why am I such a stammering clutz with Dominique? Geez.

The rest of the ride was in silence, listening to Black Pumas, Colors, a cool mixture of jazz, blues, and contemporary rock. The silence is fine with me; I just wish I didn't make things awkward with us.

"I'm sorry," I blurt out of nowhere.

"For what?"

"I don't know, for making things awkward."

He pulls into a driveway and puts the car in park, "Look at me," he demands, but not in a mean way; in a more, I command your every move when we're alone kind of way. Which brings my body to life, feeling every fiber in my being react to three simple words. Looking up, "I'm going, to be honest with you."

"Please," I respond breathily.

"You can never make things any more awkward than they already are. I'm not going to lie; I want you; hell, I need you, but I will only go at your pace."

"So, were we intimately involved? Like, more than roommates?" I question, cutting him off.

"Yes, but I will not rush you into anything because your health and safety are more important to me than a round in the sheets. And I want you to remember. Remember the way I made you feel in my embrace, the way I felt in yours," staring endearingly into my eyes, watching the tiny flecks of gold dance around his gaze. My cheeks flush, and my heart begins to race. He takes my hand, stroking my flesh with his calloused fingers.

"Okay," is all I can think of at this moment. Because in this moment, what in the hell am I supposed to say. Like, what does he want from me? Probably the same thing I want from him. But, I need time, like much-needed time to process everything. Damn, he's making it hard. Lord knows I need him too.

"Okay, then," and without another word, he steps out of the truck, runs around, and helps me out, "Here goes nothing...."

Stepping into the foyer of my three-story home—my home, I'm overwhelmed with joy at how much it truly looks like my vision boards I created so long ago. Down from the color of the walls to the crown molding and wooden floors, it's exactly how I've always imagined. The furniture, bay windows, and, oh my gosh, I have a pool in the back with beautiful plants and bushes surrounding the screened-in porch area. I continue walking into the living room when I hear giggles in the far corner from the kitchen area.

"Welcome Home, Ms. Harper!" the young boy in the pics I just saw shouts out with pure enthusiasm and joy. He comes rushing towards me when Dominique steps in front of me, protecting me from the apparent over-zealous collision.

"Remember what I told you?" Dominique chastises the young boy.

"Yes, sir," the boy says so sadly. "Sorry, Ms. Harper. I've just missed you so much," the boy confesses with conviction and heart, spreading his arms wide to show me how much indeed.

"Harper, this is Lucas, my son," Dominique introduces.

"Yes, I recognize him from the photos," I say. "Hi, Lucas."

Looking confused, "You don't remember me, Ms. Harper?" Lucas asks disappointedly, shifting his gaze from me to his dad and back to me.

"I'm afraid not, but I would love it if you would help me remember. I can't believe I would forget such a handsome face," and he blushes at the compliment. It's so weird that these people know so much about me, but I don't know anything about them.

"I surely will," grabbing my hand and pulling me to the large sliding doors. "This is where we spend most of our time together," flinching a little at the tugging, Dominique realizes it because he takes Lucas' hand and ushers him away from me.

"Oh, no. He's fine. He didn't hurt me."

"I know, but buddy, we must be gentle with Ms. Harper. She's still a little hurt, okay?" Dominique starring into his son's eyes, the same eyes he possesses, with such affection.

"Oh, man. I did it again. I forgot, dad. I promise it won't happen again. Promise," crossing his heart.

"I know, buddy. No promises needed. Here, let's let Harper head to her room so she can get settled for dinner," and in that very moment, my stomach starts to growl.

"I guess I'm a tad bit hungry now that the meds have worn off completely."

"Here, we can't let that happen, or you'll be in excruciating pain," grabbing my things and guiding me to the stairs.

"I'm a tough girl; I'll be okay." We reach the stairs, and things just got real; how the hell am I going to make it up there? So much for being a tough girl... "If memory serves me right, I think there's a guest bedroom down here. Any way I can stay down here for a couple of days?" I ask Dominique, knowing my memory is shot right now.

"Baby girl, it's your home. I'm the guest. You tell me, and I'll prepare whatever you need," he states so matter-of-factly, so firmly.

"Yes, I forgot just that quickly. I think I better stay down here until I'm strong enough to make it up those stairs," pointing to the windy stairs.

"Sure thing. I'll bring all of your things down here."

"Thank you."

Dominique guides me into the guest bedroom on the first floor. It's pretty significant for just a guest room. It has a huge walk-in closet, bathroom, study area, and bay doors leading to the pool area.

"Wow! This is gorgeous."

"Well, you did design it. So, thank yourself. You did a remarkable job."

"Thank you, self," I state proudly, and we both burst out laughing. Bending over and grabbing my waist, "Shit, that hurts."

"It's time for your meds, but you have to eat first. So freshen up, and we'll take care of your things later. I'll go make us some dinner."

"Wow, and he cooks. How did I get so lucky?"

"Trust me, I'm the lucky one," Dominique Staes proudly, walking out, back straight and chest out; confidence swirling all around him.

IT'S DAY TEN IN THIS HOUSE, AND I'M ABOUT TO LOSE MY MIND. Like, I'm bored to death, still don't have my memory, and for some odd reason, I can't leave this prison. Dominique won't tell me anything. He won't tell me why these people are after me. What do they want from me? Or even…

"Ugh… I've got to get out of here!" I yell to the rooftops. Storming out of my room, I run straight into Dominique, almost knocking myself down in the process.

"Whoa, there. I gotcha," Dominique grabs me by the shoulders to steady me on my feet. "What's the hurry? He asks.

"I can't take it anymore. I have to get out of here. Do something; anything," I confess, finally. Letting myself voice my mind.

"Phil in the Park event is being hosted in Forsyth Park. I think we should go. We're both on edge, and I think it will do us some good. It's a beautiful day. Why not?" Dominique suggests as I straighten myself.

"Really? I can leave?" I ask with enthusiasm in my bones. I'll do anything at this point.

"Sure. Let's pack a lunch and grab our blankets and chairs."

"How about I make the lunch, and you grab the blankets, wagon, and chairs? Wait, do I own lounge chairs and a wagon?"

"Yes, you do, and that sounds like a plan."

I head to the kitchen to make my shrimp and crab ceviche. I know Dominique would love it.

After making our goodies, I pack everything in the cooler and picnic basket. But, of course, we can't forget the IPA beer and wine. I then head to the SUV, where Dominique has packed all of our necessities. Apparently, I have a Buick Enclave, white in color.

"Ready?" he asks.

"Yep! Hold on, where's Lucas?"

"He's staying at a friend's house from school."

"Oh, okay. Then we're ready."

We hop in the car and head downtown to enjoy some pleasant jazz music and the wonderful citizens in the Savannah area.

"Wow, such a huge turnout! This is great!" I exclaim.

"Yes."

People are sprinkled everywhere with picnic tables, blankets, chairs, and crazy movie themes. Some people went all out with their pieces, like dinner tables set for eight and then some...lounge chairs, plants, lights... it's crazy. I've never witnessed such spectacular fun in my life.

This is awesome.

I'm so glad Dominique thought of this. I needed to get out. With my memory loss, I've felt captive in my own brain, my own body, my own house.

As I spread out on the blanket and Dominique sits in the lounge chair, I watch him cautiously. His eyes scan the crowd as if he's waiting for something or someone to pop out at any moment. He's so tense, so ridged. I need him to loosen up; enjoy the music like everyone else.

"Dominique?"

"Yes," he answers without shifting his gaze.

"Are you looking for someone?"

"Uh, no, not really. Just being aware of our surroundings."

"Are you expecting something to happen?"

"Look, the guys who are responsible for putting you in that hospital are still out there, lurking. So I need to make sure you're safe and protected."

"I'm aware, but do you think they'll attack me with all of these people out here?"

"Yes, he's done it before," he states firmly.

"How do you know this? Why won't you tell me what's going on? Don't I deserve to know everything?" I probe because why not? This is my life, too.

"What do you mean? I've told you what you need to know."

"That's further from the truth, and you know it. Look, I might've lost my memory, but I haven't lost my inquisitive nature," sitting up, trying to capture his attention. Music playing around us, and people enjoying the atmosphere. "Please look at me."

"Harper, you—I—look, it's very complicated."

"It's only complicated because you're making it complicated. You can tell me what's going on, but you refuse to, and I'm sick of being left in the dark," I throw back.

"Okay, okay. I will tell you everything when we return home. You're right. For now, let's enjoy the music and the food you've made. I promise I'll be one hundred percent in due time."

"That's all I ask," reaching into the cooler to prepare the ceviche and crackers. "Would you like wine or beer?"

"I'll take a beer. And Harper?"

"Yes," glancing up to meet his gaze.

"Thank you." I smile a soft, warm, and gentle smile, then continue to serve the both of us. I know he's right about my safety, but I am sick of having to look over my shoulder for someone I have no idea who they are or why they are after me. I just want my life back, go back to work, grieve my father, and live my life the way I intended. Is that too much to ask for?

CHAPTER TWENTY-FOUR

DOMINIQUE

WALKING through the front doors of the precinct, I head to the captain's office. It's time for me to get over my shit and stop these pricks.

"Ms. Hadley, can you let the captain know I'm here to speak with her. It's of extreme importance."

"Sure. Sit there, and I'll let her know you're here," standing and walking into the captain's office, Ms. Hadley leaves me in the waiting area. "Corporal Parker, she will see you now," she announces after a few moments.

"Captain Sadie, I'm in. Whatever you need from me, I'll give you one hundred percent. I give you my word," I state as I walk into her office. Captain Sadie is stern, but she's always fair.

"Let me ask you, why now? Why do you want to join SIU now? What's changed?"

"This Orangejello person is after people I love, and I need to know why."

"What do you mean? I need to know everything in order to sign off on this transfer."

"Okay, ma'am. I'll tell you everything, but I need to know that I won't lose my job after I tell you."

"You know I can't promise you that. So what have you done?"

"DOMINIQUE, YOU TOLD ME YOU WOULD TELL ME WHAT'S happening. So what are you hiding?" Harper cries out with so much rage, anger, and hurt upon my return home. I've confessed everything to Captain Sadie, and by God's grace, I can keep my job and am now a new investigator for SIU.

"Okay," finally giving in. I can't hold on to this burden forever, and I don't want her finding out from anyone else about my past. She deserves the truth.

I guide her to the sofa, but she refuses to sit. But it's not for her. It's for me. I'm about to unleash every heartache I've held in, and I'll need the support more than she will. But finally, with all the strength I can muster, I will lift this burden from my soul.

"Two years ago, I was seeing a woman named Dayna Pierce. She was an officer alongside Ethan and me. She was everything Keisha, my ex-wife, wasn't, strong, smart, courageous, passionate, and more. She was able to take my mind off the shit Keisha was putting me through and then some. You see, we made a pact to make each other feel something, anything other than the pain we were suffering. She wanted to get over her ex, and so did I. The night she was killed, she wanted to end what we were doing because I couldn't give her what she wanted. I couldn't give her—" Unable to finish, Harper hands me a glass of whiskey. Hell, I didn't even notice she left my side; even then, she knew what I needed.

"Please continue. I must know and understand what I'm up against."

Taking a swig of my drink, I continue my demise, "Dayna was pregnant with my child when she was killed, but not only that, she was raped and beaten weeks before her death. They tortured her, and I never found out why. And now, I find out the person responsible is this Orangejello guy who was shacking up with Keisha and terrorizing my son."

"How is this related to me?"

"The day you were kidnapped, beaten, and shot was the same day you killed Keisha."

CHAPTER TWENTY-FIVE

HARPER

"WHAT? NO, WHAT DO YOU MEAN?" I ask in disbelief.

"You and Perez were responding to a person with a gun pacing in the middle of the street. That person was Keisha, my ex and Lucas' mom. When you and Perez tried to engage, she started shooting, but before you could stop the threat, she shot Perez in the neck. You then shot and killed Keisha, but then some guys took you. Now the captain and lieutenant are sure the guy responsible for all these cases is Orange-jello. So I've asked permission to join the SIU team to assist in bringing him to justice."

"Wow," taking everything in.

"Yeah, it's a lot to process. But I promise you, I'll be here to get you through it all."

"How can you promise that? How can anyone promise that?"

"Because I will be there even if it kills me. And that, Harper, I can promise."

"How can I help?"

"If you can keep an eye on Lucas, it would put my mind at ease."

"I mean at work. How can I help at work? I'll always be here to take care of Lucas."

"You're still not allowed to return until you complete your physical fitness test. The department needs to know you're fit for duty."

"I have to do something, anything." I'm bored out of my mind.

"There may be something, but it will involve you staying in the precinct or at home. Are you up for that?"

"Yeah. I can stay here and watch Lucas and work on this case."

"Okay then. I'll talk it over with Lt. Hall. Hopefully, I can get the buy-in to bring you on while you're on light duty. But you mustn't overdo it. The doctor said you must give your memory loss time to come back. You can't rush it."

"I know; I know." I just want my life back, doing something mean-ingful for a change.

I WAKE UP DRENCHED IN SWEAT. MY BED, CLOTHES, everything, soaked and wet. I carefully get out of bed, freezing to death. My body is trembling so hard I may break something. I make it to the bathroom when my head begins to throb fiercely.

Bending over, I feel pain pulsating through my head, causing me to become queezy. Flashes of blue lights surround my vision, then a cold, wet floor in a cave of some sort. I hear voices, but the pain I'm feeling is overpowering me with fear and deafening my hearing. The pain in my stomach, "Oh God," the pain in my head.

"Ms. Harper, are you okay?" someone asks in the distance.

"I—I need some water," I begin to vomit on the floor. "Please..."

"Okay, Ms. Harper. I'll be right back," a little boy responds. I think it's Lucas, but the pain and nausea have overpowered my other senses; I can't tell.

I hear voices, but I can't make out who it is. Then, vomiting again, I feel someone pick me up.

But, no, the pictures I keep seeing. No—flashes of a woman in the middle of a street.

Then voices in a locker room arguing about a girl. Did they say, Dayna? I don't know. I'm not sure. Ugh.

Then Perez, lying there, bleeding from the neck. No, Perez! Please get up. Please.

And daddy, oh God, daddy!

My daddy died and left me with a crazy amount of money.

The letter.

I never read the letter. It's in my locker. I need to read the letter.

Dominique, the incredible sex we had. The passion we felt for one another. His hands, fingers, body, absorbing every part of me.

Lucas, oh Lucas, such a joy to have in my life.

I clench to whoever embraces me in their arms. The coldness across my forehead. The soothing touch on my arms.

Someone is taking my wet clothes off, and I let them. I can't do it on my own. The pounding sensation in my head is killing me.

"Please. Take the pain away. It hurts so much."

"Here, take these and drink a glass of water. You'll feel better after you get some rest," a voice tells me. A robust masculine voice. A voice I recognize.

"Dominique? Is that you?"

"Yes, baby girl, It's me. I'll take care of you." With that, I drift to sleep with no more care in the world.

―――――――

MY EYES FLUTTER OPEN TO TOTAL DARKNESS. THE BLINDS pulled shut, and the lights turned off. I hear soft snores coming from the seating area. My mouth is dry as the very cotton in my toiletry bag. I reach over to my nightstand for my glass of water I always place there.

But, of course, I knock it over as my eyes try to adjust to the darkness, "Shoot."

Hearing movement in the seating area, "Here, I got it. Lay and relax. You've had a rough night," Dominique insists.

"Okay," giving in because he's right. I'm exhausted.

"Here, drink this," Dominique handing me another glass of water.

After taking a sip, I sit up in bed and turn the light on, setting the glass on the nightstand, "Dominique?"

"Yes."

"I think I had some flashes or episodes of events that I lost during my incident. But I'm not sure if they were memories or my mind playing tricks on me."

"Tell me what you saw, and maybe I can help you sort through what's real and what's not."

"Okay," taking another sip of my water. "I saw a woman lying on the street, and then I think I saw Perez bleeding from the neck, laying on the ground next to the patrol car. But we weren't supposed to ride together. Henry got hurt earlier that day, right?"

"Yes, that's correct."

"Is he okay? Both, I mean?"

"Yes, both are okay. Harris took care of Henry. He's home with her, and Perez, well, he's still in the hospital. But he'll have a strong recovery. I visit every day."

"Okay, good," taking another sip of water. "I heard voices in a cave of some sort. I'm still a little confused on that part, and then...." I pause for a moment.

"Take your time. You don't want to push yourself too much."

"I know. It's just—it was so many little flashes, and it's hard to put the pieces together," taking a deep breath, I continue, "My daddy. I'm the one who found him."

"Yes."

"He left me a crazy amount of money, and I don't know why or how. The letter. He left me a letter. The lawyer told me to read it, but I didn't. It's in my locker."

"Harper, sweetie, I'm not aware of a letter or any money. You never discussed that with me. But you did tell Lucas that your dad gave you something, but you weren't sure how to feel about it."

Looking up from my glass of water, "I was mad at you. But I'm not sure why," pausing for a moment to gather my thoughts. "Hold on, we were intimate multiple times, weren't we. Not just once?"

"Yes," his jaw tensing from anger or fear. I'm not sure.

"What is it? Please tell me," I plead.

A sickening silence drifts between us, with a chill flowing across my arms. I'm terrified of the answer, but I have to know what happened between us.

"I hurt you, and before I could apologize—" he takes a long pause, dreading the following words coming from his lips.

"I was kidnapped, shot, and loss my memory," finishing his sentence.

"Yeah."

"So, how did you hurt me," thoroughly curious. I don't want to be mad at him. He's done so much for me so far. How can I be upset?

"Let's just say I put my big foot in my mouth. I said something that I didn't mean or didn't know that I didn't mean, and I've regretted it ever since then."

Impatiently waiting, "What was that?"

"After having mind-blowing sex, I mean out of this world type of love-making, I said the words that no woman, no person wants to hear...."

"Jesus Christ, you're killing me."

"We can fuck without catching feelings...."

"Wow," is all I can muster at this moment. I can see why I got mad; boy has it been eating him alive.

"Yeah, I know. But, we ended up having sex again. It was different, more like a need and we were okay, I just wanted to do more, say more. Show you, you mean more than just a fuck."

"Well, to be fair. I never thought I would have time for a relationship. Always been a casual type of girl anyways, no hard feelings."

"But that's further from what I want, what we deserve," grabbing my hands and placing them in his lap.

"I'm not going to lie. When I woke up in the hospital, all I wanted was for you to touch me, caress me, and make me feel anything other than what I was feeling. Hell, I want that now. But I also know you've been holding back because of what happened, and I respect that," releasing my hand and turning from me. "No, please don't shy away. We'll figure this out," taking his hand in mine, ensuring things will be different.

"I do have a question."

"Anything."

"Do you remember anything from the kidnapping?"

And the moment, lost, just like the wind passing through the night.

"I remember hearing voices and being in some sort of cold, wet, dark room or cave or basement."

"What about the voices? Could you make them out?"

"No, sorry. I don't remember. Wait, I remember talking to April, our dispatcher. Maybe she knows something or heard something."

"Bet. I'll speak with her tomorrow. Just thought we could figure this thing out. Why this Orangejello guy is after officers?"

"Well, did y'all do a background on him? Like a true deep dive from the moment he was conceived?"

"I'm sure SIU have; I've just haven't seen the work-up."

"Maybe that work-up will have the answers you're looking for."

"Yeah, maybe."

"Call Lt. Hall. I know he's covered every basis, and he wanted you a part of the team for a reason."

While Dominique calls Lt. Hall, I head to the kitchen to make chicken kale soup. It feels good to get some of my memory back. The struggle has been real and so frustrating. I know I still have a long road ahead of me, but at least I have something to look forward to now.

Dominique walks out of the guest room and heads towards the kitchen as I cut the carrots, potatoes, and chicken breast.

"Hey, Lt. Hall said he has the full work up. He's stopping by the house in an hour."

"Perfect. Dinner will be ready then. Hopefully, he has something we can put our finger on."

Hopefully.

CHAPTER TWENTY-SIX

DOMINIQUE

I HEAR a knock on the door as Harper sets the table. Lucas is staying at a friend's house tonight, giving us plenty of time to chat. I still haven't told him about his mother. Hell, how can I?

Opening the door, "Hey, L.T., how's it going?"

"Good, hoping you can crack this code. We're at a stand-still for now."

"Bradshaw is here as well. We'll see what we can do," letting him in. "I hope you brought your appetite. Bradshaw made chicken kale soup."

"Chicken kale, what?"

"Soup. Don't knock it until you try it."

"Whatever you say. My wife tries to feed me that healthy shit, too," chuckling to himself.

We enter the kitchen area where Harper has the table set for three and a bottle of white wine.

"Hi Bradshaw, how are you recovering?"

"I'm recovering well, and it's good to see you and know who you are."

"That's wonderful news."

"Here, sit there. Let's eat and see what we can find in the workup."

"After dinner, we head to the back porch. With the heaters, I think I installed; it feels great out here."

Lt. Hall hands over the paperwork. We divide and conquer. After about two hours, Dominique notices something.

"Look at this," taking the paper he's looking at, I take a look at it.

"What am I looking at?"

"Orangejello was in a long-term relationship about two and a half years ago," Lt. Hall states. "I can't believe I didn't see this before. Orangejello is his middle name. His government name is Robert Orangejello Holmes, Junior. His father was a piece of shit and still is, but now his son has taken over the business and is, in my opinion, worse than his father."

"Wait, the person he was in a relationship with was Dayna Pierce?"

"Yeah! That's the connection."

"So, are you saying Orangejello wanted to torture Pierce because they were in a relationship, and she broke it off?" Harper asks.

"That's exactly what I'm saying. He was very abusive towards her. There were so many reports, but she never wanted to press charges. She tried leaving him that night with the assistance of the Domestic Violence Unit, but he got to her first."

"Fuck!" I shout. "This is all my fault."

"No, Dom, it's not. You couldn't have known."

"What did you say?" I question Harper, snapping my head up.

"This isn't your fault. You couldn't have known."

"No, what did you call me?"

"Um, Dom, I think."

"Yes, you called me Dom. That's what she used to call me."

"Am I missing something?" Lt. Hall asks.

"Yes, sir. I have a lot to explain, I'm afraid, and now everything makes sense.

CHAPTER TWENTY-SEVEN

DOMINIQUE

LT. HALL CALLED Captain Sadie and Wilson. They're headed here to Harper's home. Our relationship will be out in the open for the world to know. Am I ready for that type of pressure? I know I've already explained myself to Captain Sadie, but Captain Wilson and Lt. Hall? Am I prepared for this type of intrusion in my personal life? Can I admit to the world that I'm falling hard for Harper? That I completely fucked up with Dayna and possibly ruined Keisha?

Can I?

Is Harper ready?

I have a few moments to run this by her before our lives change forever.

"Harper."

"Yes," she turns at the mention of her name.

"Can I have a moment?"

"Sure." We head to the spare room. "Lt. Hall, we'll be right back."

"Of course. I'll wait for the captains to arrive," he offers.

"Thanks," I respond.

Harper and I enter the guest room, and I swear I cannot only feel my heart beating out of my chest, but I can also hear it increase rapidly. The air has thickened around us, and I feel uneasy about all of this.

"What's up?" Harper asks, oblivious to the severity of this situation. She can't remember the unspoken rule of not dating co-workers on the same shift or unit. But now that I'm at SIU, we can be together.

"I have to explain something to you before the captains come."

"Okay," dragging each letter and syllable out.

"When the captains come, we must be honest about our relationship."

"Was it a secret?" she asks.

"Well, not really, but sort of. We're not allowed to date within the unit. If we do, one of us has to transfer, which I wasn't completely honest with you."

"What do you mean? What were you dishonest about?"

"Well, I told you I've been transferred to SIU, but I actually requested to go to SIU."

"Oh, I see." The doorbell rings before we can finish. "I guess it's time to be honest," shrugging her shoulders as she walks out.

"Fuck!"

"Hey, Captain Sadie, Captain Wilson. We're sitting just this way," Harper guides everyone into the living room.

"Hey, Caps," both Lt. Hall and I say in unison.

"So, I hear y'all have a lead on the officer-involved shooting," Captain Sadie states.

"Yes, ma'am," I answer. "We think Orangejello is after me."

"How so?" Captain Wilson asks.

Taking a big breath here goes nothing or everything...

"Start from the beginning," Lt. Hall encourages. Harper sitting silently with no discernible expression on her face. I can't figure out what she's thinking at the moment.

"I was in an arrangement with Officer Pierce—"

"What kind of arrangement," Captain Wilson cuts me off.

"In a sexual agreement."

"Oh, I see," he nods me to continue.

"We were, well, I was still married to Keisha, and Pierce was leaving her boyfriend. At the time, we were tackling our frustrations through sex, and for three years, it was working. But Pierce wanted more, and I, well, I wasn't ready for another long-term relationship. I was fine the way things were, but she wasn't, and I had to let her go. She wanted to go back home with her parents, and she told me all of this the night she was—"

"Killed," Captain Sadie finished for me.

"Yes, ma'am."

"Parker didn't know that Pierce was trying to flee from her boyfriend. She was being abused, and she finally had enough. We're thinking her pregnancy gave her the strength to leave because she knew her boyfriend would eventually kill her and her unborn child," Lt. Hall continues.

"She knew," I asked, startled by this revaluation.

"Yes, she knew. She was trying to finish her last shift, say bye to some friends, and then leave. I just didn't know she was with you," Lt. Hall points in my direction.

"Yeah, we kept it quiet, but I didn't know about the baby and I assumed she didn't know either."

"So, how is this related to the recent kidnapping of Bradshaw," Captain Sadie asks.

"Pierce was involved with Orangejello before me. It was him who was abusing her," I answer.

"Ohhh, I see," Captain Sadie states with understanding.

"We believe Orangejello figured out Pierce was with Parker and killed her and all of those people in the process to make it look like something else. He then started seeing Parker's ex-wife, finding out she was his wife through friends she started hanging out with. He got her hooked on drugs, and she fell hard, eventually convincing her to kill Parker because he got custody of their son. What she didn't know was Parker responding on a call when the reports came out about a woman with a gun a couple of months ago when Bradshaw shot and killed her."

"But, how does Bradshaw come into play?" Captain Wilson asks.

"Bradshaw and I were—or are in a relationship now," I confess.

"Okay, we're following, but how did he know y'all were dating," Captain Sadie pipes up.

"There has to be someone close to you or both of you who is feeding him this information," Lt. Hall suggests.

"But, who?" Harper finally speaks up with genuine curiosity and concern in her tone.

And the lightbulb lights up and pisses me off even more, "What the fuck?"

CHAPTER TWENTY-EIGHT

HARPER

THE PURE DEVASTATION I witnessed in Dominique's expression was unimaginable. It was heartbreaking, and I was so afraid to go to him and comfort him around these people. Now, granted, they are our command staff, but I don't know these people like I've gotten to know him, and from what Dominique told me, I didn't want to make things worse for the both of us.

But he called what we had a relationship, like a real relationship. I'm feeling so many emotions; it's making me all giddy inside and confused as hell. I should be upset that people are trying to kill me, but I'm not. I genuinely believe Dominique will do everything in his power to protect Lucas and me.

I need to talk with him, but he, the lieutenant, and the captains are huddled up in the corner like it's some kind of secret.

"Hey, I would like to know what's going on. This threat kinda includes me," rolling my eyes.

"Baby girl, you're right. We should be including you, but we also don't want to overwhelm you."

"He's right. A traumatic brain injury is nothing to play around with," Lt. Hall states. "Trust us, we know."

And I believe the lieutenant when he says those unspoken words.

DAYS HAVE COME AND GONE. I'VE BEEN GOING TO PHYSICAL therapy every other day to regain my strength. Running on the treadmill in my gym, allows me the strength to climb all flights of stairs in my home without getting winded.

Dominique moved all of my stuff back into my room, and still, I couldn't help but want to make a move on him. I've been craving him even more than ever, and it's about to drive me crazy.

Continuing my three miles, my mind drifts back to the conversation the Captains, Lieutenant, Dominique, and I had the other day. I don't know everyone on our watch, but Dominique thinks it's someone we work with feeding information to the Orangejello guy for some reason. It's hard to believe someone so close to you would betray you like that, but what do I know. I can remember some things, but not everything, so who am I to judge or speak on the matter.

All I know is I need a thorough fucking, a glass of wine, and a nice hot bath. In that order. Is that too much to ask?

I head to my room, take a hot shower, and head downstairs to make something to hold me over until lunch. Thinking of Dominique's hands all over my body, him impaling me into my bed, taking my breath away one more time, is becoming impossibly hard to ignore.

"Hey, baby girl. Whatcha thinking about?"

Startled and blushing, "I--I...what?" stammering over my words. My heart races a thousand miles a minute.

"Use your words," Dominique teases me.

I playfully slap him on the arm, knowing damn well it didn't phase him not one bit. "I am. You just scared me," needing time to come up with a lie.

"Right," taking my last slice of avocado toast with fresh tomatoes marinated in mojo.

"Hey, that's mine," I whine.

"Stingy with your thoughts and your food. Whatever should I do?"

"Mind your business and make your own food," I snap back.

"Why would I do that when yours is completely available?" he smirks.

"Playful today, I see."

"How do you feel about having a drink with me at Jazz'd Tapas?"

"Are you sure you want to be seen with me out in the open?" I question sarcastically.

"Fair, I deserve that. Look, the command staff already knows about us, and I've already switched units. I'm ready."

"I'm just a little thrown. You've made so many decisions for us, and you haven't discussed any of them with me before making them."

"You're right. I should have run the SIU thing by you and told you about opening up with my past before I laid it out to everyone for scrutiny."

"Dominique, I want you, hell, I need you. But you have to be one hundred with me. No holding back. Give it your all."

And before I can say another thing, I'm lifted up, Dominque kissing me vigorously and carrying me to the guest bedroom. He sets me down gently on my feet.

"Are you sure?"

"Are you?" I counter. "You're the one who attacked me." And before I know it, my clothes are lifted off me and thrown onto the floor. He gazes at me with such intensity it makes me ignited within.

"I'm ready!" is all the understanding I need before I give this man all of me. Something I've been waiting on for weeks. "Slide up; I want to cherish every inch of your glorious body," he demands.

I do as he says, watching him peel off his clothing one item at a time, making me wet from anticipation.

"Open your legs wide. I want to see all of you."

I do as he says, making me feel completely exposed to him and only him, yet I'm not embarrassed by the bruising and scars on my stomach, arm, and legs. Instead, I actually feel beautiful because of the way he's absorbing every move I make. Taking me in completely.

"You look so beautiful, Harper. I've waited for this moment for so long."

"Then why wait any longer?" I question incredulously. "You're killing me. Please…" And that's all it takes before my clit is taken completely. Plucked, sucked, thighs cherished, caressed by this wonderful creature.

It doesn't take long before I'm gushing in Dominique's mouth; he's lapping every spill of my essence, making me feel unbelievably incredible.

Coming down from my intense high, Dominique crawls over me, gliding his enormous, pierced dick over my clit, giving me shivers and goosebumps on my arms. My God, he's so big. Will I even be able to take all of him?

I think Dominique notices my apprehension because he tries his darndest to soothe the tension in my body.

"Baby girl, this will hurt, but I need you to tell me if it's too much, okay?"

"Please, Dominique, I need you now," pushing all thoughts of fear away and allowing pure pleasure to take over my senses.

"I need to know that you'll tell me if it's too much."

"Of course, I will. Now, please, before I lose my shit."

Finding my opening, stretching me completely, it hurts like hell, but I am damned if I utter one word to stop this exquisite, no, profound moment. Memories flooding back, giving me life I didn't think I had, "Oh God!" I scream out.

"Are you okay?"

"Yes, yes, yes!" Dominique's penetrating me over and over again, going deeper and deeper. Memories flashed before my eyes of the moments I shared with him, tears welling behind my eyelids. "Oh, Dominique. I remember! I remember!" I cry out, holding on for dear life. I let him fill me completely, thrusting in and out repeatedly, muffling my cries with kisses.

"That's it, baby girl. Give me another," he grunts out loudly. "I want to feel you come on this dick."

"Please, harder, Dominique. Please," I beg once more because, face it; this is hands down the best sex I've ever had, like ever. And, of course, he obliges my request, giving me everything he got, not holding back. My nails slicing down his back as I reach my highest climax ever.

"Oh, God, Harper! Fuck!" he bellows in complete bliss. "Got damnit, girl!"

He rolls off of me, and just when I think he's going to get up and leave, he pulls me into his arms and kisses me tenderly, like he never wants to let me go. Something I never expected; not from him.

"Shit," I sit up in a panic.

"What is it?" Dominique sits up with me, alarmed at my outburst.

"We—we didn't use protection. I don't remember taking any type of contraceptives," I state dismayingly.

"Baby girl, you can't have children, remember?" he responds meekly. "We're both clean. We touched bases on the subject before making love the last time," he reassures me.

"Oh, I see. I'm so sorry. The moment, it's gone because of me."

"Baby girl, we could never lose that moment even if we tried; not anymore," comforting me as my tensed muscles relaxes. "I'll cherish this moment we shared forever." And with that confession, we make passionate love once again; nice, slow, and intensely deep.

AFTER HOURS OF CUDDLING, I BEGRUDGINGLY PULL AWAY, "Are we still going to Jazz'd Tapas?"

"It's solely up to you, baby girl," kissing my hair.

"I can stay like this all day, but Lord knows I want to bust out this joint," we both burst out laughing.

"I guess we're heading out," kissing me tenderly on the neck. "Oh, did I hear that you remember everything?"

"Yep, everything!"

"Thank goodness. So, all it took was a spin in the sheets? Damn," he smirks a little. "Why didn't I think of that earlier?"

And with that, we make passionate love a third time.

I won't be able to walk for a week at this rate.

CHAPTER TWENTY-NINE

DOMINIQUE

IT TOOK SOME TIME, but Harper and I managed to get out of bed, get dressed, and get ready to head to Jazz'd Tapas.

She looks so mesmerizing, I wanted to fuck her again, 'cause lord knows I can't get enough of her. Harper doesn't even realize how much she affects me, but hearing her beg for me, wanting me, needing me, broke me entirely down. Finally, I couldn't hold back any longer.

I called Katie, Ethan, Henry, and Martin to see if they wanted to join and to figure out who's the feeder. Perez is still in the hospital, so I've x'ed him off the list. The doctor said he'll be released in a couple of more days. Ethan declined, something about being under the weather, somewhat suspicious, but I didn't push the issue. I didn't want to expose myself just in case I should be looking at him harder, even though we'd been friends since middle school. So, it's just Harper and me, Katie and Henry, and Martin.

"Dominique, are you ready?" Harper calls from the kitchen.

"Yeah, just checking on Lucas, and I'll be right down."

"Say hi for me," she yells out.

Dialing Lucas' number, he picks up on the second ring, "Hey buddy, how's it going?" I had to get him a new phone after everything going on. He doesn't know about his mother yet, and the threat to our family isn't going anywhere anytime soon.

"Great, Dad! We're having a blast," he answers with enthusiasm. "We've beat the new level on FortNite and working on the next. Did you need something? I have to get back."

"No, buddy, just wanted to hear your voice, and Harper says hi."

"Okay, Dad. Love you, and tell Harper I love her too." And then the line disconnects.

He loves her. Wow. I guess I wasn't prepared to hear that. Not now, anyway.

I head downstairs to meet up with everyone. We decided to take one vehicle because parking is hectic downtown. But the person I can't keep my eyes off is Harper.

She's wearing skin-tight jeans with washed, cut-out patches in different areas, with pink tights underneath. She's wearing a cut-off hot pink tank with my favorite nickname on it, Baby Girl, tied in a knot in the back with no bra underneath, showing her perky nipples through the fabric. She has on hot pink pumps, which bring her to eye level, and holly fuck, the black and pink makeup she has around her eyes and her long ringlets draped around her shoulders are literally bringing me to my knees.

Hot damn!

"Hey, y'all. Everyone ready?" I ask but keep my gaze on Harper.

"Yep," everyone responds at once.

"Let's do this," Henry shouts.

"Yes, let's," Harper responds. "I've waited too long to hang out."

———————

WE ALL PILE UP IN HENRY'S NAVIGATOR AND HEAD TO CITY MARKET, somewhere I haven't been in a long time. City Market is where my life changed completely, and reframing from going down there for the past two years hasn't really stopped the nightmares. So, why not take a chance. Besides, Harper is definitely keeping my mind occupied.

Just her presence gives me the strength I didn't think I had. I can do this—with Harper by my side.

"You should have worn a dress," I whisper in her ear.

"And why is that Mr. Parker?"

"So, I can do this." I swipe my finger over her folds protected by her jeans and panties. She pants lightly, thrusting her hips for more.

"Oh, God! Poor choice of wardrobe," she utters seductively.

"Yep." I nibble on her ear. We're in the very back, so no one can hear us over the music. Through her cloudiness, she returns the favor with a firm caress of my now rock-hard length. I moan into her ear, forcing my fingers beneath her jeans, finding the one thing that will undo us both. I fuck her with my fingers as she stroke my dick. I continue my assault, bringing her to her climax. I know she's a screamer, so I inhale her moans with my mouth, dipping my tongue deep inside, allowing her to come undone on my fingers.

Once she climbs down from her release, I remove my fingers, place them in my mouth and make her watch me suck and gravel all of her essences from the tips of my fingers.

Moments later, Henry finds parking in the Whitaker parking garage, and we all pile up in the elevator leading to the middle of Ellis Square. It's a Saturday night, so it's thick downtown. Since the shooting, the

Chief has decided to shut down all streets surrounding Ellis Square and City Market. A good decision, I think, on his part. Foot and vehicular traffic can get congested in this small area.

We make it to the top and are hit immediately with live music and laughter from people enjoying the beautiful night. It's a little chilly but not too cold, giving us a great vibe of the night. Couples sitting on the benches and bridal parties screaming for joy. There are people from all walks of life enjoying the atmosphere of this Fall evening. The different bars compete for attention with a unique genre of music and sounds.

I decide to take Harper's hand into mine, letting the whole world know she's mine and only mine. She glances at me over her shoulder, and just the simple twinkle in her eye and that smile makes me wonder why I ever thought this wouldn't be a good idea.

"I see y'all finally gave in?" Katie chants, waggling her eyebrows.

And at that acknowledgment, everyone starts for Jazz'd Tapas, not adding any more pressure on us to discuss.

Once we make it downstairs and walk through the threshold of the quaint jazz bar, my senses are attacked by different aromas of dishes and handcrafted drinks.

Sweet notes of the harmonica, electric guitar, and smooth bass drums liven the entire room. The vocalist is nothing short of an artist, singing, "Hey lady, yo husband been cheatin' on us...."

As we make our way to a lounge area in the corner to accommodate all of us, we're surrounded by red and green walls with colorful paintings on them. There are different party groups, from bridal parties to birthday parties.

Our table has a snakelike and gold-infused bar finishings with every liquid pleasure imaginable behind the bar. The bartenders are outstanding; you'd think they were a part of your personal experience.

I signal for a waitress when Harper sits next to me, allowing me to inhale her sweet perfume. The atmospheric elements of the room are so seductive, her nipples hardening under the thin fabric, making my dick twitch a little, and I have to adjust my boxers.

Whispering in her ear, "You look beautiful tonight."

Entwining her fingers with mine, "So do you."

"God, the things I want to do to you right now."

"Down, boy, we have company."

"And?"

"So, you're okay with the whole world seeing your toys?"

"Now, now, now. You should know better than that. I don't like to share," I exhale in frustration. "Fine, tonight you're mine again and again and again," and at that revelation, Harper shivers under my command as the waitress interrupts us.

"Hey guys, my name is Amy. I'll be serving you tonight. What can I get y'all?" Amy asks in her thick southern drawl.

"I'll take a Mojito," Katie announces.

"Any crafted beer you have on tap for me," Henry states.

"I'll take a raspberry lemon drop martini, please," Harper expresses.

"I'll take an old fashion," I say.

"And, I'll take a Shirley Temple. I guess I'm the designated driver with no date," Martin utters. "It sucks being the fifth wheel."

"She will not be the designated driver. So get her a lemon drop as well," Harper states. "Besides, Henry drove, so you should be able to enjoy yourself."

"Yeah, Martin. I got y'all. I'm only having two beers, and then it's water and red bull the rest of the night," Henry assures.

"Thanks, guys," Martin thanks.

"Now, to find you a date," Harper chimes in. And everyone starts laughing.

I take this opportunity to chat a little with Henry. I'm not close to him, so I need to feel him out. "Hey Henry, how are you holding up after the injury and all?"

"Doing much better. Thanks for asking, and Katie has been instrumental in ensuring my well-being is taken care of, if you know what I mean," bumping me in the shoulder with his elbow.

"So, you and Katie are finally an item?"

"Just between you and I, the sex is off the charts, but I think she's holding back, something to do with her past. But I won't push her until she's ready. I'm just glad to get her any way I can," he admits.

"I know the feeling."

"So, how are things with you and Bradshaw? I see things are getting kind of serious," he inquires.

Not wanting to give him too much, "We're coming along. It's funny, you know."

"What's that?"

"I've been on y'all watch for two years now, and I never took the time to get to know any of you, and now we're—let's just say, I'm thankful to have all of you on my team."

"Alpha Watch is family. We look out for each other, no matter the circumstances."

"I'm starting to see that."

"I do have a question about your boy, Ethan."

Piquing my interest, "What's that?"

"I've seen him with some shady people in the last couple of months. I'm not sure if you know; it just doesn't sit right with me."

"What do you mean? What did you see?"

"Just that we've made some significant arrests on some dope deals, and with each, I've seen him having side conversations with them. And then, just the other day, he was in the backyard of one of the houses we hit. He said he grew up with them and didn't know we were watching them, but it was a little odd. Or maybe he's right. I shouldn't have said anything. It could be pure coincidence. Sorry man, I shouldn't have brought it up. It just didn't sit easy with me, you know?"

"Yeah, I heard ya. Maybe a coincidence indeed."

Amy brings all of our drinks, and for the rest of the night, my eyes are on Harper, but my mind is conflicted with the information just shared with me. So many questions and not enough answers.

Interrupting my thoughts, "Dom, dance with me," Harper insists. That name again. I don't even know if she realizes what that name does to me.

Taking my hand into hers and trying her best to pull me up, I oblige her request and usher her to the small dance area. I wrap my arms around her waist and her arms around my neck, getting dangerously close to each other.

The band is playing 'Something In My Heart' by Michel'le, and this song right here, does something to me, mixed with being so close to Harper, smelling her delectable scent, and her calling me Dom...damn.

The song switches to the Weeknd's 'Call Out My Name,' and it damn near forces me to fuck Harper right here, right now. Her ass pressed against my dick, causing unneeded but much-wanted friction on my shaft. Watching her bend over in those heels, displaying her perfectly plump ass for only me. As she glides her perfect body up mine, I turn her around to face me.

"Harper, baby, let's get out of here," I whisper in her ear tenderly.

She glances up under her lashes, and my God, I pray she completely understands, with my erection growing harder and harder, pressed against her stomach, my hands feathering her arms, thighs, ass...Jesus. I can no longer contain myself.

"Let's—" kissing her furiously, taking her taste completely in, depleting the little strength I have.

Pulling away with a loud smack, I have to steady her on her feet. Then, I pull her towards our sitting area, "Hey guys, we're going to cut out early. Y'all good?"

Henry nodded, knowing exactly the meaning behind my statement.

"Are you sure?" We're not even two drinks in," Martin pouts.

"We'll stay, y'all, two love birds have fun," Katie responds.

"Ohhh, I get it now," Martin perks up, and with that, Harper and I head for the exit.

Harper pulls out her phone to get an Uber when we run into Ethan. "Hey man, I thought you were under the weather," I state, confusion in my tone. Something ain't right.

"Uh—I was feeling better, so I decided to join the party," he stutters slightly, obviously catching him off guard.

"Hey Ethan, the rest of the team is downstairs. We're heading out," Harper states. "Glad you're feeling better."

"Oh, yeah. Much better. I think I ate something bad that did not agree with me," Ethan offers.

"Well, see you soon," Harper waves, then takes my hand into hers, and for the first time in Ethan and I's friendship, I notice a hint of jealousy in his gaze and a tad bit of fear and sorrow.

"Ethan, man, you sure you're alright? You don't look so good," I question, throwing him a bone in this moment. If he's planning on doing something tonight, I'm damn sure gonna make him feel guilty as hell about it.

"Naw, man, I'm good. I'll catch y'all later," he responds, then turns his back to the stairs without another word.

What. The. Actual. Fuck?

CHAPTER THIRTY

HARPER

I'M SO horny right now, but Dominique's mood changed the moment we ran into Ethan...What could have possibly happened from the dance floor to the top of the stairs in front of Jazz'd Tapas?

Like what?

I think this Orangejello guy is really getting to him; putting him on the edge or something. The only way he can get over this mess is if he talks about it. He's been keeping so much to himself. It's not fair to him or me.

"Dom, is everything okay?" I ask meekly so as not to set him off.

"Yeah, baby girl. I'm fine," he deadpans.

"No, you're not. Something changed back there. What's going on with you and Ethan?" I push. Running his hands through his hair, I can tell he has a lot on his mind. "Maybe, I can help," I offer.

"He's the one. He's been fucking betraying me all this time," he spits out as we continue to ride in the back of the Uber.

"What do you mean? Do you think he's been trying to get us killed? Do you hear yourself? That's preposterous. He's your best friend."

"And he's hiding something. He couldn't even look me in the eye," he spits out.

"But, to kill you? Me? Dayna? It can't be true," I try my hardest to disagree in the tiniest voice I've ever had.

"Think about it. He's the only one who knew about Dayna, me, you, and Keisha. Damnit," he snaps. "I have to figure this shit out. What happened two years ago for all of this shit to happen. Something happened, and I intend to find out sooner than later. Our lives depend on it," he exclaims.

The driver pulls up in front of the house, and we step out of the car as I send the driver a tip through my app, "Thank you so much. Have a good night," I tell the driver.

"You're welcome, ma'am. You too."

Before Dominique makes it to the front door, I grab his hand, forcing him to stop for just a moment, "I know you're upset, but for one night, can we forget about tomorrow and focus on right now?" I plead with everything I have.

He glances down at me with conflicting eyes. The gold flakes dancing across his irises. He takes a deep breath and wraps his arms around my waist, pulling me closer to him. God, I love his touch; so strong and masculine, yet delicate and soothing. He brushes my hair from my face and just stares for a moment.

"If anything happened to you—" not finishing the sentence, but I know exactly what he means because he means everything to me.

"Dom, please make love to me," and without another word, he swoops me off my feet, crashing his lips to mine as we make our way through the front door. Then, never losing connection, he kicks the door shut, toting me up the stairs in his strong arms.

I didn't realize how much I needed him, depended on him, until this very moment. It's him that I desire and want. It's him that I crave and lust for. We make it up to my room when he gently sets me down on the bed. He scans my body with his lustful eyes, making me utterly slick between my legs.

He bends over me, tugging on my nipples, and oh my God, it shoots lightning to my core. "You're so goddamn responsive to me and so needy. Fuck you turn me on, Harper."

"Dom, I need you."

"Fuck Harper, do you have any idea what that name does to me," he questions through gritted teeth.

"Um, no. I can stop—"

"You'll do no such thing," cutting me off. "I love hearing you call me Dom. You've awakened something fierce inside of me."

"Okay," I muster while he softly wrench on my nipples, with purposeful pain, creating pleasure and desire.

"Take your clothes off. I want to see you. All of you."

I do as he says, slipping out of my heels, then sliding my jeans down my curves.

"Fuck, you're wearing pink lace panties too. Jesus, Harper!" He stalks over to me, bringing my arousal to new heights I didn't even think were possible. He bends on one knee, lifting my leg over his shoulder. He slides my panties to the side, running one finger over my wet slit. "Fuck, Harper, you're so wet for me."

Trembling, he holds on to my thigh tightly, "Oh God. Please," I beg. Removing his finger and sucking my essence right off his fingers makes me orgasm right here, right now, "Ah," I scream out.

"That's it, baby girl." He begins to lick me, laying his tongue flat on my pussy, causing my clit to react to every movement he makes. He sucks and nips, causing me to come once again. "Take off your shirt, baby girl." As he licks me clean, I manage to lift my shirt off, dropping it on the floor. "Baby girl, I want you on your hands and knees, ass completely up. I want to see that pretty fat pussy."

I do as he requests, but I can't see him. The anticipation is killing me, "Please," I plead.

"God, baby girl, your juices are sliding down your leg. You are so wet for me." After what seems forever, he finally touches me, causing me to leap forward, "Where are you going, baby girl?" He grabs me by the hips and finally gives me what I've been craving. Thrusting inside of me, I nearly hit the headboard. Dominique has to pull me back to steady myself. I feel everything in this position. Every curve, his thickness, his girth. He continues to thrust inside me over and over again. Harder and harder, slower and slower, then faster and faster, causing me to squirt all over the damn place.

"Dom—" he flips me over without any heads up.

"I want to see you, baby girl. I want to watch you as I pleasure you." He enters me again, but it's nice and slow this time. So slow, I dig my heels into his ass, urging him to speed up. "Wait, my needy vixen. I'll give you what you want in just a moment. I want to feel you completely."

"But I want to feel you come," I whine.

Between each sensual thrust, "You will. You will," he moans softly in my ear.

He picks up the speed, thrusting harder and harder, giving me exactly what I yearn for, "Yes, yes, yes," I scream in complete ecstasy. "Oh, my God!"

And with that, he releases his seed inside me, filling me completely. Then, collapsing on the side of me, wraps me in his arms, blanketing me with his warmth, kissing me so delicately on the nape of my neck.

"I love you, Harper," Dominique whispered in his low husky voice, catching me completely off guard.

"You...what?"

"I love you, baby girl," repeating himself, because face it, I had to hear it again to make sure I wasn't dreaming.

"You love me?" I question a little harsher than I wanted to.

Turning me in his arms, "Baby girl, I'm not saying this to scare you. I'm saying it because I may not get another opportunity to express my feelings. How I truly feel."

"I—I'm not scared; I just—I'm not sure what to say. This is so new to me; I mean, I just got my memory back, and—"

"Harper, baby, please stop. I'm not expecting anything. Just letting you know how I feel. If you're not there yet, I understand. I have no problem with waiting," pulling me to him, kissing me softly on my lips. I want to return the same sentiment so badly, but I'm just not ready yet. Not yet.

But I do wonder, "Why me?"

"What do you mean, baby girl?"

"I mean, well, I've never been in a serious relationship, like never. I just, my parents weren't the best role models, and I always promised myself to never fall so deeply for someone, and then they hurt me," I utter, praying that he understands.

"If you don't mind me asking, what happened? I mean, with your mom and dad?"

"I don't. Not anymore anyways," taking a deep, much-needed breath, I spill my deepest secrets. "When I was six years old, my mom left us. Saying something about us smothering her. It absolutely crushed my dad. The day she left; is the day I lost my father too. I spent every day since taking care of my dad. Between drinking and crying every night and going to school and the academy, I was too busy to be in a real relationship. I kind of had one-night stands since the day I graduated. Never wanted to go through what my dad went through."

"Have you ever tried finding your mother," he asks, genuinely curious.

"No," I utter with such finality.

"Will you? I mean, try to reach out to her."

"No, what's the point. If she wanted me, she knew where we were. My dad refused to leave for years until the home went into foreclosure, and that's why I was so mad at him when he left me all that money. Like, he was rich, and I spent my life trying to take care of him, and he never said anything, not one thing," I say with anger in my tone. I didn't even realize I was crying until Dominique started wiping the tears away.

"Baby girl, I didn't mean to bring up old wounds."

"I know. You needed to know. It's only fair I share my darkest fears when you've shared yours."

"You mentioned a letter. Do you think that will provide the answers you're looking for?"

Shrugging my shoulders, "I don't know. In a way, I want to read it, but then I'm afraid to find out what really happened. Was I that bad as a girl for her to want nothing to do with me? Did my dad hurt her, cheat on her, or betray her in some way?"

"You'll never know the answers to your questions if you don't read that letter."

I know he's right; I just can't right now. Not right now. I just want to lay in this bed with the hottest guy in the world and fall asleep a happy woman.

"I know," is all it takes for him to drop the discussion and wrap his protective arms around my small frame, allowing me to absorb everything in this moment.

A moment later, our breathing evens out, and we drift to sleep completely sated.

CHAPTER THIRTY-ONE

HARPER

THERE ARE SO many things I'm genuinely grateful for, but deep down, I have this nagging feeling I can't get rid of. Like, an itch you can't get to or a cramp in your shoulder you can't reach.

Even though Dominique and I relationship has improved tremendously, I still can't shake that feeling.

Dominique went to work, of course. He couldn't use any more leave time to babysit me, and to be honest, I wish I could go back to work too. But my doctor hasn't signed off on my return yet.

So, it's Lucas and me today. It's been a while since I've really hung out with him, and I really want to, like, really. I never really considered having children, and now that that option has been taken from me, I want them more than anything. But, will I be a good mother? Unfortunately, I haven't had the best role model in the world. My mom left me a long time ago.

To think of it, I need to get that letter my father left for me.

I hear a knock on my bedroom door as I rise from the bed. "Ms. Harper, are you awake?" Lucas asks.

"Yes, give me a moment," I announce back.

"Okay," Lucas responds.

I head to the restroom to brush my teeth and wash my face. My hair is a mess, but whatever, I'll make an appointment with Danyelle at B.Poise. She's been doing my hair for years. She'll get me right.

I throw my hair into a messy bun and put on a pair of white leggings and an oversized sweater. Once I look myself over, I head to the door.

I open it, and Lucas falls backward into my room. Apparently, he was sitting, leaning against my door, until I was finished.

"Oh, sorry, Lucas. I didn't know you were waiting for me here."

"It's okay, Ms. Harper. I wanted to show you something." Grabbing my hand and pulling me down the stairs, we almost trip because he's much shorter than me, and I have to lean down to keep up. "Ms. Harper, look," Lucas points towards the kitchen.

It's a complete disaster in here, but glance at what he's trying to show me. He made breakfast for the both of us. There're two bowls of cereal, with fruit and glasses of orange juice. I'm so amazed that I'm completely speechless. This is the most thoughtful thing a young boy his age can do.

"Lucas, you made all of this for us?"

"Yep," he responds with so much enthusiasm. "I didn't know how to work the coffee machine, so there's no coffee, but I made juice."

"Oh, Lucas, this is so thoughtful. Thank you so much. Here let's eat," I guide him to the table. Then, after sitting for a while in silence, "Lucas, would you like to go with me to the precinct? I have to get that important letter I told you about."

"You haven't read it yet?" he asks, confused.

"No, not yet."

"Why not?"

"Well, to be honest. I was scared."

"Why?"

"Because I may learn something I don't want to know."

"Why? I learn things all the time at school, and sometimes I don't like it, but I still have to learn them. Dad said if you don't learn, you won't know anything."

"True, it's just...I don't know."

"Would you like me to hold your hand while you read it? That's what daddy does when I'm scared of something."

"I would love that!"

"Okay. Let's finish eating, and then we can go get that letter. After that, we might even see daddy."

LUCAS AND I HEAD TO THE PRECINCT AFTER WE EAT AND clean the kitchen. This little boy has really opened my mind. Making me think and all. Like, he's right. Why am I so scared? I need to know what happened between my mom and dad all those years ago.

We took Dominique's brand-new truck since my car battery was dead. Not driving it for a while will do that. We pull up to the precinct when I realize I forgot my access card to get in.

"Shoot," I state.

"What is it, Ms. Harper?"

"I forgot my access badge."

"Oh, just call dad or the precinct. They'll let you in."

"Right, why didn't I think of that?"

"Because you're worried about that letter."

"Valid point."

I called the front desk when the receptionist, Ms. Hadley, answered, "Northwest Precinct, how can I help you?"

"Hi, this is Bradshaw. I forgot my access card. Can you buzz me in?"

"Of course, Corporal Bradshaw. Of course," Ms. Hadley answers with her hi-pitch voice.

After the buzz, Lucas and I walk through the front door. We're greeted by Ms. Hadley, who gives me a huge hug.

"Oh wow," I say.

"We've missed you so much, Corporal Bradshaw. You had all of us worried. We're so glad you're doing better."

"Thank you."

Looking down at Lucas, "And who are you, handsome man?"

"I'm Lucas. My dad is Dominique—"

"Dominique Parker," Ms. Hadley yelps with so much glee. "Oh, my gosh. You look just like him. We didn't know he had a son. He's such a mystery."

Maybe it was a bad idea to bring Lucas. I didn't think about Dominique being so private with his life. I hope he doesn't get mad at me.

"Yep, that's my dad!" Lucas responds so proudly.

"What can I help you with, Corporal Bradshaw?"

"I need access to my locker. I have some personal items I need to retrieve."

"Sure, right this way," Ms. Hadley guides me. "Oh, hold on. I forgot my keys." She heads back to her desk when Ethan approaches us.

"Hi, Uncle Ethan," Lucas greets.

"Hey, buddy. Whatcha doing here?"

"Ms. Harper needed to get something. Have you seen my dad?"

"Yep, he's right in there."

Lucas takes off running, "Slow down, Lucas," I yell over my shoulder.

"Yes, ma'am!" Lucas responds back.

Once he's out of earshot, "So, you and Parker?"

"Hun?"

"If you can, hun, you can hear."

"Right. What about Parker and me?"

"Y'all an item?"

"I think you know that already. You two are boys, right?"

"I would think so."

"Right!" This convo just got awkward.

"I just thought we might hit it off."

"And why in the world would you think that?"

"Because, well, that one time...."

"What one time?" thoroughly confused.

"We fucked remember?"

"What?" completely taken aback, "No, we didn't."

"Yea, we did. You just never bother calling me back."

"What in the hell are you talking about?"

"Don't act like you don't remember. You fucked me and then used me to get to my boy."

"Wha—"

"Got them!" Ms. Hadley interrupts. "Let's head to your locker. Oh, hi, Corporal Ethan. Did you need something?"

"Nope, nothing Ms. Hadley. Bradshaw, until we meet again," flashing me a disgusting yet devilish grin.

What the fuck? Ethan walks away before I can say another word.

Ms. Hadley guides me to the lockers, oblivious to what just transpired, where she assists me with opening my locker. I find the letter, fold it, and put it in my back pocket.

"Thank you so much, Ms. Hadley. I appreciate it," taking her hands into mine.

"Of course, sweetie. We're all rooting for you. Oh, and I do have a few forms for you to sign so you can get your short-term and long-term disability kicking in so you can pay some bills. I know they should be piling up by now."

I didn't even think to ask about my bills. Shit, has Dominique been paying all the bills for me?

"Yes, thank you. I totally forgot I had to sign for my checks."

"No problem. We got you covered. Corporal Parker took care of every-thing else."

Wow, I had no idea he's been keeping up with my paperwork. I don't know what to say.

Ms. Hadley and I head to her desk when Dominique and Lucas stroll down the hall. He's so handsome in his uniform. It's the tactical uniform with an outer vest, blue khaki pants, and a polo shirt under-neath. It looks like he has a hoodie draped over his shoulders. His eyes light up when he sees me, taking me in completely with his gaze. The little dimple on his cheek enhances his beautiful, enchanted smile.

God, he's so breathtaking. I still can't believe he's mine.

"Hey, Harper! What a pleasant surprise."

"Hi. We didn't mean to interrupt," I begin to explain. "I came by to get a few things from my locker, and the weirdest thing happened, but I can't discuss it here," I whisper softly into his ear as he brings me into a hug.

"Sure. We'll talk when I log off. I should be done with my shift in a few."

"Daddy, daddy, daddy. Can we go to Mellow Mushroom for dinner? Please, daddy? Please," Lucas whines.

Chuckling, "Harper, would you like to join us?"

"Sure!"

"Okay, Mellow Mushroom, it is! Let me finish up on a couple of cases, and then I'll head over. Harper, do you remember where it is?"

"Yep! I remember. Lucas and I will head over and grab a table before it gets too busy."

"Yay! We're going to the Mellow. We're going to the Mellow," Lucas sings and chants while running in circles.

And we all chuckle at his carefreeness. I'm unsure how to break this news to Dominique about Ethan and his delusional statements, but I vow to be honest, even if it threatens everything we've worked hard for.

"Ms. Harper, let's sit over here in the corner. Dad always wants to see who's coming and going," Lucas states as we enter the Mellow Mushroom. I like knowing my surroundings as well. It's a cop thing, something I miss every moment of the day.

If memory serves me right, Mellow Mushroom has the best pizza in Savannah. They inspire local artists with paintings and live bands.

They are known for their homemade crust and stone-baked pizzas with bold combinations of fresh toppings. My dad used to take me here all the time. I just haven't been here since they remodeled over the summer.

Lucas and I take our seats when a young girl approaches us with menus. She looks like a SCAD student, which we have a lot of in the downtown area of Savannah.

"Hi, my name is LJ. I'll be your server today. Can I start you off with drinks?" LJ asks.

"Yes, it'll be three of us. We're still waiting on someone. I'll take a glass of white wine. Buddy, what would you like?"

"Do you have Root Beer Float?" Lucas asks.

"Yeah, we can make a Root Beer Float," LJ responds.

"Ms. Harper, can I please?" Lucas begs, batting his puppy dog eyes with gold flakes floating across the irises. He looks just like Dominique at this moment. How can I say no to that adorable face?

"Sure, why not?" I agree.

"Yes!" he exclaims.

"And for your other guest?" LJ asks.

"He would like a crafted lager beer on tap."

"We have a local lager on tap, Southbound. It's delicious," LJ offers.

"Perfect."

"Awesome, take your time looking over the menu. I'll be right over there," LJ points to the bar area. "If you have any questions."

"Thanks, LJ, will do." She then walks away.

"Ms. Harper, did you find the letter?" Lucas asks as LJ walks away.

"I did. It's right here," pulling the letter out of my pocket.

"So, are you gonna read it?" he asks impatiently. Lucas has no idea how much this letter will affect my life, our lives. What's in this letter can change everything. Before I can respond, Dominique strolls in, and all of my fears and doubts wash away. "Daddy!" Lucas shouts. "Over here," waving Dominique over. "Here, you can sit by Ms. Harper. I know you like to watch everyone too."

Such an intuitive young boy. I love that about him.

"Hey, my two favorite people," Dominique greets us as he takes his seat next to me. I get a whiff of his masculine scent mixed with coffee and whiskey, and oh my gosh, he's making my heartbeat pick up just a notch.

"Hey," I casually say in a husky voice I didn't think I had. I seriously don't know how to act around this man.

"Guess what, Daddy?" Lucas interrupts my inner embarrassment.

"What?"

"If I tell you, then you're not guessing...duh, Daddy," Lucas responds.

"You're right, buddy...um, let me see," Dominique pretends to think really hard.

"You're taking too long, Daddy. I'll just say it. Would you ask Ms. Harper out on a date?" I spit my water all over the table while Dominique sits stunned in place.

"What was that, buddy?" Dominique manage to ask after gathering his wits.

"I really like Ms. Harper. She plays with me, helps me with my home-work, cooks and cleans for the both of us, and you look at her like the guys in the movies. You never looked at mom like that, and I under-stand why. You love her dad, and y'all should go out on a date," Lucas explains. How in the hell did he come up with all of that. How does he even know about love or dating or looking at someone like in the movies? Has he been thinking about this all this time?

"Buddy, do you realize what you're asking?"

"Yes, sir. I do. Ms. Harper, do you like my daddy?"

"Uh, yes, Lucas, I do," I respond hesitantly because, face it, I have no idea what the next question will be.

"Daddy, do you like Ms. Harper?"

"Yes, Buddy, I do, but—"

"No, don't do that, Daddy," Lucas cuts Dominique off. "You always put me first, never thinking of yourself," Lucas whines. "I want you to be happy, Daddy, and I know Ms. Harper makes you happy."

After what seems forever, we're interrupted by LJ, our waitress. She approaches us, and the moment she sees Dominique, she plasters this weird-looking smile on her face, ignoring Lucas and me all together, "Hi sir, I'm LJ. I'll be your server. What can I get you?"

Clearing my throat, "Um, I would like the pepperoni and sausage pizza with jalapeños. Lucas, what would you like?" I feel Dominique squeezing my thigh underneath the table. Probably because he knows I have a smart-ass mouth and I managed to keep my mouth in check after the blatant rudeness.

"I like barbeque with pineapples, please," Lucas sings.

"And Babe? What would you like?" I state, feeling a little brave, letting her know he's all mine, so back off.

"We'll take some hot wings. I love both those choices, so I'll steal a slice from y'all," Dominique states.

"Oh really? Who said I wanted to share?" sliding his hand up my thigh and between my legs, shutting me right up.

"That'll be all," Dominique states without even looking at her. She walks away, ultimately defeated. Serves her right. How dare she hit on my man. Wow? My man? Did I just say that? Yep, I think I did!

AFTER EATING DINNER, JOKING AROUND, AND MAKING SMALL talk, we all head home. Dominique in his unmarked vehicle, and Lucas and I in Dominique's truck.

"Ms. Harper. Do you think dad's mad at me?"

"No, why would you ask that?"

"Well, he never answered my question about y'all dating and...."

"And what? You can talk to me."

"Well, some kids were talking in school the other day."

"What were they talking about," trying to drag whatever is eating at him.

"Well, they say my mom is dead, and now I don't have a mommy. That's why I want you to be my mommy," he deadpans.

Holy fucking hell!

"Sweetie, would you like to speak to your dad about this?"

"No, I don't want to upset him. He's gotta lot of stuff to worry about at work."

"I see. But I really think he would want to hear how you feel about everything."

"I just don't understand why he didn't tell me. I'm a big boy now."

"Yes, you are, but it's complicated. I think your dad wants to protect you no matter what and shelter you from bad things."

"But he can't, Ms. Harper. The kids at school are horrible."

"Yes, they can be."

"When I thought they were lying, I looked it up on the computer. They were right."

Shit! Fucking technology.

"Look, we're almost home. We can sit with your dad, and I promise I'll stay by your side if you get scared. Deal?"

"Yes, ma'am. I guess."

Shit, Dominique isn't going to handle this well at all. But I can certainly be there for both of them.

CHAPTER THIRTY-TWO

DOMINIQUE

LUCAS REALLY THREW me completely off guard with the matchmaking. I had no idea he was even thinking of setting Harper and me up. Something must be up with him. This isn't him.

I pull up in the driveway, allowing Harper to pull my truck into the garage. We need to get her a vehicle, but she can continue driving the truck for now. She's been a godsend to Lucas and me; I could never deny her anything. Lucas is correct, I do love Harper, but I have to talk to him about his mother...sooner than later.

We all enter the house, and I turn off the alarm. Lucas and Harper are very quiet. I have to find out what's going on with my son.

"Hey buddy, can I talk with you for a moment? Harper, do you mind?"

"Actually, if it's okay with you, Lucas would like to say something to you, and he would like me to be present."

"Uh, sure. Why not," something is up.

"Well, dad...some kids were joking around the other day and said my mom was dead."

And my world comes crashing down before me with such solidity. The breath leaves my lungs with such force, my jaw ticking with every second, and yet, I still remain calm while he finishes.

"I didn't believe them, so I looked it up on the internet. Why didn't you tell me?"

Stunned, I just sit there speechless.

"It's not your dad's fault for not telling you. It's mine," Harper states. My head snaps in her direction in bewilderment. What is she about to do? "Lucas, you remember when I got hurt and lost my memory?"

"Yeah."

"Well, the reason I got hurt was that I responded to a horrifying call. When my partner and I arrived, a woman was waving a gun at people and screaming. When I tried to help her, she started shooting her gun at my partner and me. She hit my partner, but I was able to duck and cover, but I also returned fire, shooting the woman. I was taken by some bad guys who tried to hurt me, but your dad here saved me," Harper pointed my way. "You see, the woman I shot was later identified as your mother."

She's taking the blame. All of it. I can't let her do that.

"I didn't know how to explain to you that your mother is no longer with us," I add. "I was scared of what it might do to you, son."

"Mommy used to wave her gun all the time, scaring me and hitting me with it. So I prayed one day that it would kill her."

"You what?" I spit out in complete disbelief.

"Yeah, Mommy and that man were bad people. They scared me every day. I prayed that they would both die and you would take care of me, but then you met Ms. Harper, and I wished she would be my new mommy," he explains.

Holy shit. How did I not know this about my own child? How have I been so blind that my own child was suffering, and I allowed it? How?

"Daddy, I'm not telling you to be upset; I'm being truthful because Ms. Harper said something today," he continues. Harper's head lifts in confusion. "It's a daddy's job to protect his kids and shelter them from bad things, but this wasn't your fault, daddy, and I don't want you to be upset—"

"Buddy, I'm not upset with you. I wanted to tell you about your mother. I just didn't know how," I try to soothe him the best I can. "And I certainly did not know how you felt about her. Ms. Harper is correct. It's my job to protect you, and I failed. And from this day forward, I vow to always protect you," I promise, a promise I intend on keeping.

"So, will you ask Ms. Harper out now?" he asks, changing the subject.

I look into Harper's eyes and see the wheels turning in her beautiful gaze. I take her free hand in mine and ask the question I should've asked a long time ago, "Will you go out with me?"

I've been hiding my relationship with Harper all this time and didn't need to. I should've known Lucas would see between the lines, behind the lies and secrets. That kid is intuitive, truly.

As I GET DRESSED FOR OUR SECOND DATE, BECAUSE, FACE IT, Jazz'd Tapas was our first, we just never made it to the eating part, I contemplate everything that happened thus far.

We still haven't figured out where Orangejello is hiding and who's helping him. Just because my former partner and best friend, Ethan, has been acting a little shady doesn't make him a cold-blooded killer. He's always been there for Lucas and me and vice versa. But I do believe something is going on, and I need to get to the bottom of it.

After putting on a nice gray button-down shirt, with a pair of dark, washed-out jeans and a blazer, I head downstairs to wait for Harper. I'm taking her to the Vault on Bull St for dinner.

After that emotional conversation with Lucas, we decided to slow things a little and date rather than fuck, but don't get me wrong, the fucking is definitely worth breaking our word. Harper is exceptional in bed, feeding my needs and wants at once. Her body molds to me so nicely; it's like she's made for me only.

Grabbing a drink from the fridge, Harper enters the living area, and my God...she takes my breath away every time. She has her hair in large curls down her back, with a burgundy dress so tight, I can envision her curves underneath.

To hell with going out; I need to fuck her to oblivion.

"Like what you see," Harper interrupts my thoughts.

"Here's a thought; let's skip the dinner and head straight for dessert," I suggest.

"Now, now, now...we can't give up on our word to Lucas. Besides, he's right. We both need this," she offers.

"I suppose you're right...this time," I chuckle a little. "But I can't promise not to fuck you senseless afterward.

"I wouldn't have it any other way...."

CHAPTER THIRTY-THREE

HARPER

AFTER THE MOST romantic date I've ever been on because, I must admit, I've never been a dating type of chick; we fucked like horny dogs mating for hours, which felt like days. I could barely walk the next morning. And my va-jay-jay, holy fuck...I seriously don't think it will ever be the same. Dominique has ruined it for any other man to enter this pussy.

Just remembering the way he cherished every part of me, running his hands down my body like he couldn't get enough of me.

And when he entered me completely, oh...my...gosh...it was like heaven seeping through my very soul. Like, he was my other half, the piece I'd been missing for so long. Every guy I've fucked doesn't compare to how Dominique makes me feel.

I'm sitting on my back porch, surrounded by birds chirping in the bushes, dogs barking in the neighborhood, and wind blowing gently as the weather changes from fall to winter and back to fall because, Savannah weather is bipolar.

It's November, Thanksgiving is around the corner, and I have yet to prepare for Thanksgiving dinner or read the letter my father left me.

Dominique is at work, and Lucas is at school, so it's just me, the birds chirping, and the dogs barking.

I open the letter, unfold it, and take a deep breath before reading the first line...

Pumpkin, the nickname dad gave me a long time ago but stopped using it when mom left.

Clearing my throat,

PUMPKIN,

Where to begin? I have so much to tell you and little time to explain it. So, I'm just going to rip the Band-Aid off. Your mother was part of the TRAP unit with the Savannah Police Department, undercover, prior to meeting me. She resigned when she became pregnant by your real father, Robert Holmes. Robert was one of her targets while working undercover. He became obsessed with your mother so much he raped her every night, not knowing she was undercover. She begged to get out, but her supervisor in the TRAP refused because they didn't have enough to bring down the entire operation. Ignoring her complaints was just the beginning. I still don't know what that entailed. She never talked about it. She just said she was handling it.

After she got out, I promised to love her and raise her baby as my own, with love and care. Little did I know, she was planning to leave us. It was later that I realized she was still undercover, just using us as a pawn for her needs. There were signs, but I ignored them in hopes that she would return to us. It was too often she said she never wanted children and how you and I were in the way. I just brushed it off as depression, but it was more than that...way more.

You see, MaryAnn returned when you were fifteen in hopes of getting us back. She repeated over and over again she never meant the words she slapped me with all those years ago. She said she was trying to keep us safe, but didn't know any other way to do it, so she left us both. I didn't believe her and pushed her away because I didn't want her hurting you again... not again. I had so much anger built up and could not forgive her.

It is now that I believe her.

There have been strange men lurking around, sitting in cars, walking through our yard, and I even saw one enter our home. So, I purposely let our house go into foreclosure. I had to protect you at all costs.

You're probably asking yourself... how or what, or why. Yes, Pumpkin, I was an alcoholic, but I was lucid enough to figure that someone was trying to kill us both. I just thought they would, or I would by alcoholism. I'm sure you've figured out which by now.

Pumpkin, if you're reading this letter, you're in danger. I left my entire life savings in hopes of helping you establish a new life, a better life than I gave you. We lived poorly because I didn't want them to find us, and I knew I had to protect you. I just couldn't put the bottle down. I had no more willpower.

In short, Pumpkin, you were loved by your mother, and if she's still alive, find her, listen to her, let her explain something I never gave her the opportunity to do, and love her. She can help you stay alive and live your life but also watch your back because your real father has been trying to find you for a long time now. He's pure evil and will do everything in his power to destroy your soul if you let him.

I know this is the cowardly way to give you this information, but face it, I haven't been much of a man. I love you always, and please forgive me for failing you all these years.

Love you always, Pumpkin.

Dad

Holy fuck!

CHAPTER THIRTY-FOUR

DOMINIQUE

THE SQUAD AND I ARE SITTIN' up on a dope house right now, waitin' and anticipating the moment to hit the house. SIU has been investigating this home on the Eastside for months, and now we have a search warrant to hit it.

There are three teams, and I'm part of the second, the Breach Team. The first team surrounds the house, and the third makes the arrests and makes sure everyone receives medical attention.

Once we get word to move in, it happens so smoothly and methodically fast, I question if we've missed something. I give it to SIU and SWAT; they got these optics down to a science.

It's my first one with the team, and I feel pretty good about how they maneuver and operate.

We were able to make ten arrests in this search warrant, recovering one hundred pounds of weed, eighty pounds of heroin, and several grams of fentanyl.

All this time, I didn't give a damn about this unit, but this, right here, made me feel like I'm making a difference for the City of Savannah.

"So, what do you think? Something you can get down with moving forward," Corporal Briana Jones asks as we walk out the front door. She's been on this unit for years, scooping her up quickly. I don't think she did a day on the street before joining the SIU Team, and I can see why.

With shoulder-length dreads, kept neat, tats and piercings all over her arms, neck, and ears; she's short with an athletic build, with skin the color of honey. She's cute but not sexier than Harper.

"I'm not going to lie, I wasn't too keen on joining this team before, but now that I got a little taste of what y'all do, I'm game for anything."

"That's what we like to hear," Corporal Jones responds. "Citizens and officers always have a negative view of this unit until they truly under-stand what it is that we do. We're just like any other officer on the street. We want to stop crime and save lives, but we do it differently. We do it by stopping gangs from selling drugs to our youth, stopping gangs from raping our women and young girls, and stopping gangs from brainwashing our men and young boys. Of course, Gangin' is not the only way to make money, but it's certainly the easiest to get locked up or get killed," shaking her head. "I'm just glad I can save one person at a time, one day at a time."

"And that statement, right there, is the reason I became a cop."

AFTER TWO LONG DAYS OF STAKING OUT, I JUST WANT A HOT shower, a drink, and to see my little man and my beautiful baby girl.

She texted me earlier, needing to speak with me in person, but I was too busy with the search warrant. So now, I'm headed home to get a much-needed kiss from the love of my life.

I enter the home, and Lucas runs straight for me, giving me the biggest hug. "I've missed you, daddy!"

"I've missed you too, buddy. Where's Harper?"

"She's in the kitchen cooking dinner. We're making Creole ground beef, rice, and red beans."

"Wow, that sounds good and smells good."

"Just between you and me, she's been a little off since yesterday. But I cheered her up," Lucas whispers to me.

"Good job! Thanks for picking up the slack, buddy."

"Sure thing Dad. I'm a big boy now." He then takes off running upstairs.

I set my stuff down and take my shoes off at the front door. I then head for the kitchen.

"Hey baby girl, I hear you've had a bad day," wrapping my arms around her petite frame, pulling her close to me as she cooks at the stove.

Obviously startled, "You scared me," she pants.

"A penny for your thoughts?"

"I don't know where to start," responding in a tone that raises concern.

"Start from the beginning," tugging on her earlobe.

"Well, I—I read my father's letter."

"Wow, okay. What did it say?" I ask cautiously yet curiously.

"My mom was a police officer for Savannah PD, and my father isn't my father; he's my stepfather. And my real father is possibly trying to kill me. I think that sums it up," she states matter-of-factly.

Shit!

"How do you know your real father is trying to kill you? Who is he? Why didn't your father, well, your stepfather, tell you all of this when he was alive?"

"All questions I have, but no answers to them. My dad said I needed to find my mother. Oh, and my real father's name is Robert Holmes."

"Wait..."

"Yep, Orange jello dude's father...."

"What in the actual fuck!"

"My thoughts exactly."

CHAPTER THIRTY-FIVE

HARPER

EVEN IN DEATH, my father is a pain in my ass. For sixteen years, my father never once suggested that he wasn't my father nor hinted that my real father was trying to kill me.

Like, what am I supposed to do with this information? Like, what the actual fuck?

Sitting on the balcony of my room, in my comfortable lounge chair, wrapped in a thick hand-quilted blanket, I watch the wind seep through the trees, making them sway side to side in an almost enchanting way.

Dominique bought me a mug warmer, which is the best thing I've ever received as a 'just because' gift. It keeps my coffee from ever getting cold while I sit out here.

So many thoughts run through my head from my childhood, and not one memory reminds me of anything remotely close to what my dad divulged in his final letter.

I have one thing I need to do to figure this out.

I need to find my mother, MaryAnn Bradshaw, and I think I'll start with Savannah PD. Someone had to know who my mother was twenty-one years ago.

"HEY DOMINIQUE, I THINK IT'S TIME FOR YOU TO MOVE YOUR stuff into my room," I suggest to Dominique while we clean the kitchen to start cooking.

He's been abiding by our contract, and I know I haven't said the words he wants to hear; I just don't see a point in him staying on the second floor when we're dating.

He stops what he's doing and approaches me, cornering me to the counter with his arms locking me in on each side. His cool breath feather across my neck, causing chills to run straight to my core. I have no idea what I said to make him react this way, but I dare not stop him. He's turning me completely on.

"I—I can't think when you do this to me," I stammer over my words.

"I know," he responds in such a husky tone; I swear my panties soak instantly.

"I think it's a little ridiculous for you and me to be in two different rooms," I manage to say.

"I don't. It's the thrill of walking up those stairs, waiting for you to open the door, demanding your presence, a response from you, something like this..." running his fingertips down my body until he reaches my panties, and oh my God, I can combust right here, right now.

"Wha—what about...Lucas?"

"Lucas is perfectly content with playing video games in his room. Besides, I can't wait to taste you," pushing from the counter. "Let's go in the guest room."

"Okay..."

Dominique pulls me into the guest room, shuts the door behind us, and damn near lavish me before I can—

Oh my gosh...

Dominique lifts my dress, and rubs his length against my core, lubricating his shaft thoroughly with my juices. Hell, I didn't even see him take his clothes off. He then slams into me, stretching me and possibly ripping me in the process, but at this very moment, I don't give a hot damn. I'll deal with the pain later.

He slams inside me so hard that it seems he's trying to enter straight through my soul. He's so rough, so needy, so demanding. I want to give him everything he wants and needs, but I'm not sure I can live up to such a standard.

"Fuck Harper, you feel so good. I can't get enough of you."

Our bodies slapping together with sweat and sex molding between us. I feel myself building to the very peak of ecstasy; but, before I can voice my release, I come harder than I've ever come...

Dominique slides out of me and gets on his knees, and oh my goodness. He is not about to— "Shit!" Yes, he's eating my pussy like a man starving for his next meal. He's licking and, my God, making love to my delicate folds. "Yes, Dom, yes, please...."

Once he has licked every drop, he slides back inside me and makes sweet, tender, passionate love to me, and we become one.

Yes, one, because we belong together. He loves me, and I love him. Like, I genuinely love him and didn't think that was even possible. I can't love him. He will hurt me if I let all of me love all of him.

This, right here, is the purification at its highest. Something abundantly opposite from the way he just made me feel a second ago.

And then... Dominique grunts the sweetest sounds as he spills his seed inside me, never letting me go.

"HARPER, BABY. IT'S TIME TO EAT. DINNER IS READY," I HEAR Dominique whisper in my ear.

"Hun," groaning softly.

"Baby girl, the food is ready."

"Shit, did I fall asleep?" Sitting up too quickly.

"Yes, you did. I didn't want to disturb you, baby girl. You looked so peaceful," he admits as he kisses me on my forehead.

"Thank you. What did you decide to cook?" I ask as I climb out of bed and dress.

"I made steaks, grilled potatoes, and cauliflower."

"Sounds delicious." I follow him out of the room and sit at the table next to Lucas.

"Hey buddy," I greet Lucas.

"Hi, Ms. Harper. Dad, can we eat? My friends are waiting on me."

"Sure. We'll rush for your friends. We dare not let them wait," Dominique responds sarcastically.

"Sorry, dad," Lucas pouts.

Dominique says the blessings, and we all dig in. "Can you pass the cauliflower?" I ask .

"Sure. Here, tell me when to stop."

"I love cauliflower, so pile it up." And he does. "I want to find my mother," I blurt out.

"Okay," Dominique drags out cautiously. "Where do you want to start?"

"I thought to start with the police department. If my mother was a cop, then why didn't anyone ever tell me? Why didn't my father? It was only twenty-one years ago. Someone in that department knew my mother. I want to start there," I state firmly.

"Then we shall."

"You don't know your mother?" Lucas asks.

Shit. I didn't think this through. I shouldn't have blurted that out.

"My mother left when I was six years old. So, no, I really didn't know her. I never thought to look for her because I didn't think she wanted me. But then I read my dad's letter —"

"You finally read it!" Lucas interrupts me.

"Yeah, something like that. It said my mother came looking for me when I was fifteen."

"So, she wanted you!" Lucas exclaims.

"Yes, it appears so."

"Then we need to find her, dad. We have to help Ms. Harper find her mother," Lucas shouts.

"Okay, buddy. We will. We just have to figure some things out, and then hopefully, we can get the ball rolling," Dominique explains to Lucas.

"This is awesome news!" Lucas exclaims.

I'm glad one of us is happy because I am freaking the fuck out right now. I have no idea what to expect and if this is even something MayAnn is willing to do now. Fifteen years is a long time.

THE FIRST PERSON I REACH OUT TO IS LIEUTENANT JABARI Johnson. He's been in the department for over thirty years, and I know he has to know my mother.

I find him leaving Headquarters on Habersham St. He sometimes comes to the barracks for command staff meetings.

"Hey, L.T., can I pick your brain for a moment?"

"Sure, what's on your mind? But I'm afraid I'm running late for another meeting, so you'll have to walk and talk."

"This will be quick. Have you ever known a MaryAnn Bradshaw who worked on the department?"

"Um, let me think. I knew a MaryAnn, but her last name wasn't Bradshaw. Why do you ask?"

"Well, I think she may be my mother," stopping in his tracks, he looks at me thoroughly again, like really look at me.

"My God. I didn't notice it before, but you look just like her... the spitting image," Lt. Johnson reminiscences from a time before my time, it looks like. "Look, I have to head to the meeting, but call me at noon, and we can sit down and talk. Here's my card," handing me his business card with his cell number.

"What if we can meet at the Grind. How does that sound?" I ask.

"Good idea."

"Okay, perfect, sir. Thank you. I'll see you soon."

As he rushes away, I find new profound hope. Finally, I just might get the answers I need after all.

I'M AT THE GRIND A WHOLE THIRTY MINUTES EARLY, NERVOUS and getty as all get out. The moment I walked in, my senses are attacked with an aroma out of this world. Coffee beans and pastries warp through the quaint cafe with a vengeance, and I love it. I walk up to the counter to order a cup of coffee and a strawberry cheesecake cupcake. Dianella makes the best pastries in town, and I can't leave here without getting at least one.

"Hi Amanda, it's good to see you again," I greet the young server behind the counter. She is always here in the afternoons because she has early classes. One thing about Dianella, she supports the local colleges and students.

"Oh, hi, Harper. It's nice to see you again. It's been a while."

"Yeah, I got injured on the job, but I'm doing much better," I reply.

"Oh, yeah. I heard that on the news. I'm glad you're doing better."

"Thanks."

"What can I get you?"

"A large caramel macchiato with a strawberry cheesecake cupcake."

"Coming right up."

"I'll be in the corner over there," I point to an empty table near the bay windows.

"Sure, I'll bring it out to you when it's ready."

"Thanks, Amanda."

I then walk over to the empty table, sitting down with my back to the wall.

As time passes by, I watch people come and go out of the cafe. People from all walks of life, some carefree, and some worrisome. It fascinates me how people are so different yet so similar. We're all creatures of habit, and breaking our habits is hard.

Amanda approaches me as Lt. Johnson walks through the door. "Hey Amanda, you can get him anything he wants and put it on my tab. I got it."

"Sure thing," she turns to greet Lt. Johnson. "Hi L.T., would you like a coffee, or shoot, I forgot, you like tea. I can bring you a sweet tea."

"That'll be good. I'll take a sweet tea," he responds. He then sits on my side so he can see who's also coming and going as well. "So, Ms. Bradshaw. You're MaryAnn Winters' child?"

"Her name was MaryAnn Winters?" I didn't think about her maiden name. She didn't marry my father until after she left the department.

"Yes. Corporal Winters was the best undercover operative we had on the department. She could take down any organization, and I mean any one of them. She had this cool swag about her. And then, one day, she changed. I tried talking to her, but something had her so frightened she completely shut down."

Taking a sip of his sweet tea, he continues, "MaryAnn requested to be taken off the case, but the captain at the time was an asshole. Refused to abide by her request or even notice the change in her demeanor and attitude. She was terrified, and everyone noticed except the captain. He was too caught up in bringing the organization down, and the ramifications didn't matter. Corporal Winters was a casualty in her captain's demise. No one knew how bad it was until she put in her two-weeks notice, leaving the department altogether. I didn't even know she had a kid until today," he admits apologetically.

"Have you kept in touch with her?" I ask, hopeful.

"No, I'm afraid not," he responds. "But wait, she had a close friend back then in the department. What was her name?" Lt. Johnson trying to wrangle his brain. "Awe, yes, Captain Chantel Perrier. They were inseparable years ago. She may have information for you. She is a captain for Chatham County PD now. She went back there after the demerger. I bet she'll have the answers you need."

"Thank you so much, L.T. You've been such a huge help. You have no idea," giving him a hug.

"I'm just glad I was able to guide you in the right direction. If you find your mother, let her know there are people who still care about her and would love to see her again."

"I sure will, sir," not really. I just want to figure out what the hell is going on. Lt. Johnson finishes his sweet tea and gets up to leave.

"I hear some good things about you. But, of course, it makes sense now that you're Winters' daughter."

He then leaves the cafe.

Another piece to the puzzle.

I STILL HAVE A COUPLE OF HOURS BEFORE I HAVE TO PICK Lucas up from school, so I take another chance and head to Chatham County PD to solve another piece of the puzzle. My anxiety taking over, because I have to figure this out. I must.

As I arrive at the Chatham County PD headquarters, I call to give Dominique the good news.

"Hey, Dom. I found out my mother was going by the name MaryAnn Winters. She possibly has a friend who now works for Chatham County. I'm headed there now," I regurgitate.

"Whoa, slow down. Where are you going? I missed that part," Dominique asks.

"I'm headed to CCPD. According to Lt. Johnson, my mother was best friends with Captain Chantel Perrier."

"And how does Lt. Johnson know all of this?" He asks suspiciously.

"Lt. Johnson has been on the department for thirty years. So he's bound to have some knowledge of who some of the officers were back then. That's why I reached out to him," I explain.

"I understand. Just be careful. We still don't know who the mole is, and now that we know your mother might have been involved with Orangejello's father, we don't know who to trust right now. Just... please be careful."

"I will. I'll call you once I'm done."

"Please do."

We then hang up. He's right. I need to be careful. I don't know who to trust anymore other than Dominique.

As I approach the front door, I take a deep breath and enter. CCPD Headquarters is a lot small than our Headquarters, but it's so much newer than ours.

I approach the glass window and speak with the receptionist. She's young and energetic, with a pleasant smile. "Hi, how can I help you?"

"Hi, yes. Is Captain Perrier available?"

"Hold on, just a minute. Can I let her know who's asking for her?"

"Yes. My name is Harper Bradshaw."

"Okay, you can have a seat right over there," pointing to seating in the corner.

"Thank you."

I sit and wait patiently for the captain, but I am nervous as all get out. Moments later, a tall, slender White woman walks through the access door. She has terse blonde hair that really fits her because of her long thin neck. She's not dressed in a traditional uniform like most command staff would. She has navy blue slacks on with a white button-down blouse with short heels because, she's already very tall.

She has brown eyes and a smile to die for. Very attractive, if you ask me.

"Hi, Harper. I'm Chantel. It's very nice to finally meet you," Captain Perrier extends her hand for me to shake.

"Hi, Captain Perrier."

"Please call me Chantel. I hate formal titles unless I'm digging into someone's ass," she snickers.

"Okay."

"Here, follow me." She takes me through the access door using her badge. We then stroll down a hall, passing several offices along the way, until we make it to hers at the end of the hallway. "Have a seat here," pointing to a sofa against the wall. She has different paintings on the wall of sceneries of Savannah's historic squares. They are breathtakingly beautiful. "So, Harper Bradshaw. My goodness, you look just like your mother."

"I'm starting to hear that a lot nowadays."

"Yes, right. If you're here, you probably want answers about your mother."

"Yes. Anything you can tell me would be great. I don't know a whole lot."

"I see. And Ray didn't talk about your mother at all?" She asks specifically.

"No. He didn't. All I know is my mother left when I was five, so no, I don't know anything."

"I see. Well, your mother loved you very much, and the only reason she left you was to protect you. Her biggest fear was losing you, and she couldn't fathom that at all."

"But, why did she leave?"

"Because of your biological father, Richard Holmes. He was and still is the worst human being on the planet. He did things to your mother that was beyond unforgettable and unforgivable. The night before she ran, she came to see me. She was completely distraught and scared. Once I was able to calm her down, she told me that Richard was trying to kill her because he found out that she was working undercover to bring down his operation. He also found out that she was pregnant with his child, and he promised he would kill her and her child if he ever found where she was. I'm the one that convinced her to leave, but I tried to encourage her to take you with her. Start over. But she was too scared and felt Ray would do right by you and take care of you," Chantel explains.

"I get that she left to protect me. But, how bad was he?" I ask.

"He tied his victims up before torturing them on the bed or a chair. He would then cut each of their toes and fingers off with wire cutters. He would then pull each of the teeth out and make his victims swallow them if they were still conscious enough to do so. Then, if they were men, he would dismember their groin, and if they were women, he would cut off their nipples and then fuck them until they passed out. And if they still hung on for dear life, he would feed them to his wild dogs."

"My God!"

"That's only the half of it. If he found out you betrayed him, he would track your entire family down and torture them the same way, but let them watch each other be tortured. He was a sick son of a bitch, which is why your mother tried to get out. She witnessed this on many occasions, but the captain at the time didn't give a damn about her complaints or what she witnessed. He was only concerned about the drug aspect of the investigation. Not the fact that he terrorized and tortured people for the fun of it. And now, I've heard he has a son out there with a weird fucking name and the same psychopathic tendencies."

"Yes, his name is Richard Orangejello Holmes, Jr. And you're right, he's a sick bastard too," I explain. "Chantel, is my mother alive, and if so, do you know where she is?"

"Yes, she's alive, but you don't want to know where she is," she deadpans.

"And why is that?"

"Because she's still with Richard, and Orangejello is your brother."

CHAPTER THIRTY-SIX

HARPER

I RUN out of the CCPD headquarters as fast as I can until I reach the grass in the front. I bend over and vomit everything I ate this morning. And when I say everything, I mean everything.

I vaguely recall anyone running after me or stopping me. I had to get out, go somewhere, anywhere. I feel sick again before I hear my name in the distance. I'm not really sure who's talking to me, I just feel really lightheaded right now, and I'm just trying to hold it together.

I need Dominique; I need to call him. I fumbled through my purse, trying to find my phone. After tossing everything, I finally find it and dial .

"Baby girl, how was it?"

"Dom, please come get me. I need you," I cry.

"I'm coming, baby girl; I'll be there in a few minutes. Stay on the phone with me, okay?" Devastating fear in his voice.

"Okay."

"Harper? I know I just told you a lot, but I have more to explain," Chantel explains.

"Harper, can you give the phone to Chantel?" Dominique asks.

"Here, Chantel. He wants to speak to you."

Chantel takes the phone as I sit up, bracing myself on the bench I partially remember finding. I hear Chantel responding, but I don't have a clue as to what they're talking about.

It's just so much to deal with, and recovering from the brain injury isn't helping my cause. In fact, it's the reason I'm so nauseous now.

That asshole is my blood-blood brother...not my half-brother? Not my stepbrother... What the fuck was my mother thinking? How could she? Was she forced? Yes, that's it. She was forced to conceive more children from that psychopath. That's the only thing that makes sense. Please make it make sense. Please.

Get your shit together, Harper. You must hear Chantel out. You must.

As I rise to my feet, Dominique is running to my side. Man, he wasn't playing. He definitely was down the street.

"Take it easy, baby girl," Dominique encourages me. We all walk back into the building and head for Chantel's office again.

This time, I will hold my composure. I've been emotionally weak lately, and I hate this side of me.

"Harper, I know this is a lot to take in, and I know your mother is doing this to protect you, but I don't think she factored in the fact that her son is a maniac who needs to be stopped."

"So, are you saying that even now, my mother is protecting me?"

"Yes, that's what I'm saying. When he found out about you, she told him she had a miscarriage and that was the reason she left. She told him she couldn't bare to hurt him as well. So he doesn't know that you exist."

"But, what if he does?" Dominique pipes up. "What if he figured out somehow that Harper is his, and now everything happening is because of this sick fetish he has over her?"

"I see what you're saying, but how does Dayna, Keisha, and all the others fit into this scenario?" I question. "Could it be that these people are serial killers or serial rapists?"

"They absolutely are, but they haven't killed in our jurisdiction yet, only in the city limits," Chantel explains.

"How have they gotten away with this for so long?" I ask.

"Your mother, I'm afraid. When I told you, she was really good at her job...I wasn't joking."

"My God! My entire family is psychotic, and the only person who had my best interest was my drunken father, my bad, my drunken stepfather."

"No, that's not true," Chantel tries to reassure me.

"How in the world can you defend her? You're a cop, for christ's sake," my blood boiling at this point. I vaguely remember Dominique soothing me with his touch as I continue ranting. "She is violating the law every moment she's with those lunatics," I feel a bit weaker than before. "We all signed an oath...I—I—just can't with you people," slurring my words. And then I feel myself drift.

CHAPTER THIRTY-SEVEN

DOMINIQUE

HARPER AND I are back at the hospital after she lost consciousness. The doctor stated when she vomited, it was a clear sign for her to take it easy. But she kept pushing herself. And now, we're in this hospital for a second time. I've got to find a way to convince Harper to take it easy.

But how do you deny a person from learning where they came from? Her entire life has been a complete lie, and she isn't going to stop until she gets answers.

We're in a private room waiting for Harper to awaken when the nurse comes back in.

"Hi, Mr. Dominique. How are you holding up?"

"Not so good. Hoping Harper is okay."

"She'll be okay. But she really doesn't understand the meaning of taking it easy, does she?"

"I'm afraid not. Once she sets her mind on something, she moves full force, running over anything that gets in her way. But that's what I love about her. She's a force to be reckoned with."

"That she is. Well, we're just waiting for her labs to come back and for her to wake up. I don't see you having to stay overnight, but I'll let the doc make that decision."

"Thank you." As the nurse walks out, Harper stirs a little, letting me know she's on her way to waking up.

"Harper, sweetie? Can you open your eyes for me?" I ask softly.

She grunts and begrudgingly opens her eyes, squinting a little because of the brightness.

"What happened?"

"You passed out in Captain Perrier's office. I think it was a lot to take in too soon."

"Yeah, I think so too. My head is killing me.

"Well, the doctor will be in soon. Just lie back and get some rest. I'll ask the nurse to give you something for the pain."

"No, no drugs. I want to be lucid when we figure this out."

"Harper—."

"No, Dominique. This is our life we're talking about. If we don't figure this out, who will?"

"And lose you in the process? I can't. I won't let that happen. Not ever. You're my life now, you and Lucas. I'd never forgive myself if something happened to either of you."

"And I'll never forgive myself if I don't stop those nutcases."

Not being able to change her mind, I drop the whole conversation. She's right; we need to stop them; I just don't want it to be her. She has enough to deal with. But, if I can do it myself because let's face it, these jackasses are after me as well as her, then that's what I'll have to do.

And I think I know how to get it done where both of us will be on top. But first, I need to have a little chat with my dear old friend and former partner, Noah Ethan.

CHAPTER THIRTY-EIGHT

HARPER

DOMINIQUE IS MAKING the sweetest yet unbelievable love to me tonight; it brings a tear to my eye. There's something different about the way he tenderly cares for me in this moment. I'm unsure if it's because I passed out the other day or something else. But it's almost poetically unnerving the way he touches me, caresses me, cherishes me. Almost as if he'll never see me again.

After leaving the hospital, he made me promise to take a few days and get my strength back, and after everything that's happened, I had no choice but to oblige his request.

Dominique is taking his time, kissing every inch of my body, caressing my body with his firm grip. For the past minute or so, he's given my nipples so much attention I may combust in need.

He's purposely taking his time, every excruciating moment at a time, driving me completely insane with every lick, suck, nip, and flick of his tongue.

I cry out in ecstasy and desperate for more. He's made me a needy, horny girl, and I'm not afraid to beg for more.

He slowly slides down my body, leaving hot, wet imprints along the way, and sweet baby Jesus, I don't know how much more I can take.

I try to wrap my arms around him, to feel his warmth, or even run my fingers through his curly hair, and he slaps me hard on my thighs, demanding me to stay put.

"Didn't I say keep your hands on the headboard?" Dominique chastises me. "If you move again, I'll punish you."

"But—."

"No, buts, or I'll make you beg even more. Understood?"

"Yes, understood."

"Do you remember your safe word?"

"Um, shit. I'm not sure."

"Alpha."

"Right, Alpha. Yes, I won't forget."

He slides a finger into my wet pussy, and I near buck off the bed. He steadies me as he inserts two more. It feels so good; I rock my hips into his palming, trying my damnedest to get more.

I want more.

I need more.

Using his other hand to steady me, he swipes his tongue over my folds while fucking me with his fingers, bringing me to a climax I didn't think could happen with just his fingers and tongue.

"That's it, baby girl; I want you to come into my mouth. Let me taste you."

I find myself reaching for nothing in particular when I feel a slap on my folds, scaring the living hell out of me but yet making me even hornier than I've ever been.

"Oh, my God!"

"That's for disobeying me and this," Dominique slams his length inside me so hard and so rough, I scream, unable to keep my cries muffled anymore. "Fuck Harper, baby, you feel so good."

Slamming into me harder and harder, lifting my leg over his shoulder to give him even more access and me so much more pleasure, so much more.

I rock into him with every thrust, needing more and more. Our bodies fusing together, wet and hot and sticky, making me have the biggest orgasm I've ever managed to have. I feel Dominique swell inside of me, and I know without a doubt that I'm madly in love with this man and cannot see myself living without him or Lucas.

"Dom?"

"Yes, baby girl," he responds in a husky voice, still harder than ever inside me.

"I'm in love with you."

And with that confession, we go for round two, making soft, passionate love to each other until we pass out completely from total bliss.

CHAPTER THIRTY-NINE

DOMINIQUE

I HEAR the alarm beep that Harper installed in the bedroom when she had the home built. I then hear creaks in the floorboards, causing the hairs on my arms to stand tall.

"Harper, baby," I shake her gently to wake her up but not freak her the hell out. "Baby girl, someone's in the house. We gotta get up."

She sits up, completely alert. "My guns are in the safe in the closet. I also have two in each nightstand," we both get up and throwing something on.

I grab the guns from my side of the bed, and Harper heads to the closet to her safe. She pulls out two AK-47s, military style, and head to the safe for more. How the fuck did I not know she owned all of these guns.

Harper returns with two more shotguns, "which one do you want?" she asks incredulously.

"I'll take these two, pointing at the pistols and the AK-47."

"And I'll take the pistol and shotgun. They're all loaded and ready."

"Bet." I head out of the room first, with Harper on my heels. I'm so fucking glad Lucas isn't here to witness the shit that's about to go down. But, once I planted the seed, it was only a matter of time before these sick fucks pounced. We clear the third floor and make our way down to the second. I stop when I hear three distinctive foot patterns on the wooden floors. "Ready?"

Harper nods her head, yes, and we enter the threshold of the second floor. I shoot first, hitting my target on the left, and Harper bends on one knee, hitting the other two targets.

We hear more men coming upstairs and wait for them to grace us with their presence. The first three were masked up, so I have no idea who they are. The next set also has masks, but we hear men approaching from behind.

"I got it." Harper starts firing behind me when my targets approach. I miss the first one but hit two behind him. The first ducks off into one of the rooms. "I'm clear," Harper states.

"Let's move forward. I missed one of my targets." We continue forward when the last target steps out. Harper pulls the trigger, hitting him in the stomach, "Wait!" I yell.

Harper stops and realizes we just shot Ethan.

She drops to her knees, applying pressure to the wound, "What the hell Ethan? How could you?" Harper asks in disgust.

Ethan tries to say something, but it's inaudible.

"What did he say? Say it again, Ethan," Harper demands, bending closer. He whispers something in her ear as I call for an ambulance and backup.

"Dominique, it's his sister. They have his sister."

"Fuck!"

ALL THIS TIME, I THOUGHT MY PARTNER AND BEST FRIEND hated me so much that he would come after the people I love. All this time, he's been betraying my trust and letting people try to kill me, and now, I know he felt he had no choice.

But he did. He could have come to me. He could have told me what was going on. I could have helped him.

After EMS comes and takes Ethan away, Harper and I are interrogated by Internal Affairs. We have over six bodies lying in our home, and we shot a cop, a fucking cop. So, yeah. They have questions.

Yeah, he'll be fighting for his life, but damn. This is one hundred percent fucked up.

Hours pass, and Harper and I are still separated and asked hundreds of questions, like, were the weapons used, department issued? Do we know any of the deceased other than the cop? Do we know why Ethan did what he did? Did we have a grudge or a fight and didn't report it?

All fucking useless questions. I know damn well who's trying to kill Harper and me, I just need to track the fucker down, and I mean now.

Around seven in the morning, we're finally released from Internal Affairs with strict instructions to remain in our home until the investigation is clear. Yeah right, like we're going really abide by that shit.

We're not staying at Harper's house, so I booked a two-bedroom suite at the JW Hilton Hotel.

As I leave the office, I find Harper. She looks so defeated and exhausted. "Harper, let's head to the hotel to rest."

"What about—."

"Don't worry about the house. I'll take care of all the damage. I booked us a room at the JW to stay until we can find something while the repairs are being done at the house."

"You did all of that? I barely had time to think, let alone function. They asked me so many questions, and I really didn't have answers to any of them," she starts to cry. I wrap her in my arms around her shoulders, trying to comfort her as much as possible. When the doc said take it easy, I'm pretty sure he didn't mean this.

"Baby girl. I'll take care of you. You no longer have to be severely independent. I want you to depend on me. I'm here, and I'm not leaving." With that, she tucks her head into my side, and I guide her out of the building.

ONCE IN OUR ROOM AT THE JW, I RUN HARPER A HOT BATH with soothing bath salts and bubbles. Once she gets in, I call Katie and fill her in.

"I need you to come get my credit card and purchase all the necessities Harper'll need," I instruct her.

"And you?"

"What?"

"What about you? Don't you need stuff too?"

"I'll be fine."

"Nonsense. Jackson will get what you need as well. Give us a couple of hours. We got you."

"Thanks, Katie. Oh, and Katie?"

"Yeah?"

"How is he?" I don't even have to explain to her who I'm referring to. She knows.

"He's in ICU. Jackson's been sitting with him until he wakes up. And they still haven't found his sister. His poor mother and other two sisters are completely distraught."

"Damnit."

"I know. I have no idea what he was thinking." I can't tell her the truth, not until I speak with Harper first. I'm still not sure who to trust anymore.

"I do. His sisters are everything to him. If one of them is in danger, he would do anything to save them."

"I just wish he would've come to one of us. We would've helped him."

"I know."

"Okay, well. Please take care of my girl. She's been through hell and then some."

"I will."

I'll get my feisty, sexy cop back. One way or another.

I hang up and head back into the bathroom, where Harper is soaking and resting in hot water. I start stripping my clothes off and join her. She welcomes me wholeheartedly, and it's hard as fuck not to pleasure her soundly.

Harper embraces me completely, leaning into my chest and running her fingertips up and down my thighs, making it even harder to resist her.

"Dom..."

Just the yearning in her voice is making me weak.

"Yes, baby girl?"

"I need to feel you, please?"

And just like that, I lose all willpower to make love to this woman.

I extend my hand down her thighs, searching for her most sensitive part of her body. Once I reach my destination, she cries out in pure ecstasy, lifting her hips, forcing me to enter her fully.

I insert two fingers, and the moan she gifts me is so insanely cute; I continue faster, making her come undone between my legs.

Once she's released completely, I flip her over, splashing water everywhere, but I don't give a shit; I need to be inside her now.

"Baby, straddle your legs around me, open up completely to me." She does as I instruct, allowing my length to slide over her soft pussy.

As she lifts up and then lowers down on me, I enter her, and oh my fucking God, her walls are heaven to my dick. I have one arm wrapped around her and the other clenching the tub, bracing us both because, right now, I need it hard and fast. I thrust upward inexpugnably, and for the life of me, I see stars. I didn't think that was even possible. This woman makes me want to fuck straight through her, giving my all in this moment.

"Oh, my goodness, Dom!" She states in between breaths. Rocking right with me, with the same intensity as my pace, we fuck all of the water right out of the tub.

"Dom, I'm—," she says incompletely as she clings to my neck, coming harder than ever.

I continue to pump inside of her when she has no more energy to continue. She feels so damn good; I never want this to end. I thrust, and I pump, and I fuck, feeling my cum spill inside of her, and in this moment, I wish I could give her a baby, a child with her dimples and long wavy hair.

But the cruel world has once again taken something so precious from her, from us.

I RUN MORE HOT WATER IN THE BATH AND BATHE THE BOTH OF us before I lift her up and dry her with the hotel's plush towels.

She allows me to carry her to bed, where she snuggles under the covers and drifts immediately. She's been through so much I don't have the heart to ask for round two.

I hear a knock on the door, so I wrap myself in the robe hanging in the bathroom. I then head out of the room and shut the door, allowing Harper to sleep.

Opening the door, I'm greeted by Jackson and Katie.

"Hey, come in, but be quiet. Harper is sleeping," I whisper to them.

"Of course," Katie responds.

They both walk in with tons of bags. What in the world did they buy?

"Before you lose your shit, You'll need everything here if y'all are planning to be here for a while," Katie spits out before I can question anything.

"Yeah, bro. I'm witcha, but she insisted y'all needed all this shit," Jackson confirms.

"See, look," she holds up one bag. "This bag is for all your toiletries, and this one is for Harper. And the other bags are underwear, socks, bras, shirts, tights, jeans, etcetera, to include stuff for Lucas, which by the way, you didn't even mention. So, frankly, I saved your ass," she states matter-a-factly.

"Thanks, Katie, and thank you, Jackson. I don't know what I would've done without y'all."

"You're welcome," Katies says. "So, how is she?"

"She's doing better. Crashed after taking a hot bath. She needs the rest."

"I bet," Jackson states.

"So, what's next?" Katie asks.

"Well, IA told us to stand down," I respond.

"Fuck that. We have to find these sick fuckers and Ethan's sister. God only knows what's happening to her," Katie states, shaking her head.

"Yeah, I know; I just don't know how to get around the direct order. I'd like for us to keep our jobs," I admit.

"What if you get Lieutenant Hall involved? Use his team; that way, your hands won't be in the pot entirely. You'll just be a guide of sorts," Katie explains.

"Yeah, bro. That might work," Jackson pipes up with enthusiasm in his tone.

"Well, I want to give Harper a few more days to recover."

"Right, we get it. It certainly involves both of you," Katie explains. "Besides, I'm worried about Harper. I've tried calling her a few times, but she hasn't responded."

"Yeah, I usually turn her phone on silent so she can get some rest," I explain.

"Maybe, she and I can have a spa day," Katie suggests

"How about tomorrow? My treat," I offer.

"I never turn down a free anything. I'll book it and send the details to Harper and you," Katie explains.

"Bet," I agree.

"Well, babe, we have to head out. We're heading to the hospital to check on Ethan," Jackson states.

"Thanks for being there for him. I just can't right now, not now," I state.

"Oh, man, we understand. Take care of Harper. She's your priority," Jackson agrees.

"Sure thing. See y'all soon, and thanks again for all the stuff. We appreciate it."

"No problem. Let me know if y'all need anything else, and I'll be sure to send the spa details in the a.m.," Katie explains.

They walk out, leaving me in the living area with my inner thoughts, worries, and concerns.

"HEY L.T., I KNOW IA GAVE ME STRICT INSTRUCTIONS NOT TO get involved with the takedown of Orangejello and his father, but I can't just sit around. I have to do something," I confess on the phone.

"Oh, I know. I was waiting on your call. Once we got a search warrant for Officer Ethan's phone, we were able to pinpoint the different locations he met with Orangejello. We're sitting on three locations now," Lt. Hall explains.

"Thank God. I'm losing my mind over here."

"We'll keep you posted on what we find once we hit all three locations. Stay by your phone."

"Bet. And L.T."

"Yeah?"

"Thanks man. This means everything to me and I know Bradshaw will be relieved as well."

"No need to thank me. It was only a matter of time that we brought those assholes down."

I click off the phone and pace back and forth for hours before finally, I get the text.

Lt. Hall: It's over. Orangejello, his father and mother are all in custody!

Me: Thank God!

Lt. Hall: Now get some sleep and I'll let you know when you're in the clear.

Me: Bet!

CHAPTER FORTY

HARPER

I AWAKEN IN AN UNFAMILIAR PLACE, dem lighting illuminating the room. The walls are blush pink with polished marble, yet classic European elegance in such an intimate setting and escape of some sort. The decor is glamorous and breathtaking.

I hear Dominique snoring slightly next to me when I realize this isn't a dream. My mouth is parched, and I need water now, if not sooner.

Remembering every detail of yesterday, I let out a long, labored breath. "Why on earth is all this mess happening to me...to us?" I slide out of bed and head to the minibar. I need a drink.

Once I open the mini fridge, I find sodas, water, juices, wine, beer, and Dominique's favorite whiskey. He must have been shopping while I was sleeping. How long was I out? I grab a bottle of water when I see a covered dish with a sticky note that states, "EAT ME." I take the plate out and open it. It's sautéed flounder with scalloped potatoes and broccoli. Oh my, this looks delicious. I place the dish in the microwave and then pour myself a glass of water while I wait.

I can't believe he did all of this. I push the button on the microwave before it times out because it's so loud. I don't want to wake up, Dominique. He needs his rest as well.

I sit on the couch, food in my lap and water on the side table. I turn on the TV very low and flip through the channels to see what's on. I find the Hallmark channel and allow the romantic comedy to draw me in while I inhale this delectable masterpiece.

Two hours later, I went from laughing uncontrollably softly to crying my eyes out to genuinely believing in true love. It's six in the morning, and I feel like I can keep going for another few days. I throw my trash out and clean up my mess. Then head for the bathroom. I find women's and men's products lined up on the bathroom counter. Wow, most of this stuff I actually use on a daily bases. How in the world did he know this? He had to have help. I'm just thankful he thought about all of this.

I could not function yesterday. First, my heart felt like it would burst out of my chest, praying that we escape unscathed. And then, when I shot Ethan, my God, I was devastated. And his sister, my goodness. I can only imagine what he's going through, and my father, mother, and brother are all responsible for everything that's happened thus far. Such heartless assholes. How can I be related to these selfish pricks? How?

I open the closet and find men and women's clothes hanging, so I decide to check the drawers too, and yes, he thought about panties, bras, and camisoles. I'm utterly speechless at how tenderly attentive Dominique is to me. He used to be such an ass to me only months ago, and now, he has cared for me more than any man or my parents. I just want to wake him up and give him a huge hug and kiss and so much more.

I grab a black and pink matching bra set with panties and head for the bathroom without waking Dominique up. I start the hot shower and grab my shampoo, conditioner, and detangler brush. I drop some essential oils tailored to stress in the shower to calm my muscles and wandering mind. I then step in and allow the steamy droplets to run through my hair and down my body. It feels so good; I close my eyes, indulging in this beautiful experience. I so needed this moment. After my hair is completely wet, I lather my hair with shampoo until the suds are dripping down my neck and shoulders. After massaging my scalp thoroughly, I rinse the suds out until my hair is cleaned of soap. I then lather my hair with conditioner, sliding my fingers through every strand. I then take my brush and comb through sections until my hair is tangle free. I let the conditioner sit for a while so I can lather my body with body wash, cleansing every part of my skin, running my fingers over my scars which are healing nicely.

As I rinse my body, I allow the water to cleanse my hair. Once I'm done, I squeeze the remaining droplets out of my curls, turn the water off, and then wrap my hair in a towel. I then dry myself off before I brush my teeth, wash my face, and style my curls half up and half down.

I check the closet to see what I have to choose from and decide on a pair of torn jeans, a boyfriend's sweater, and a pair of white Nikes. Next, I lotion my body and put on perfume, deodorant, and my outfit.

I'm ready to conquer the world and the psychopaths I call family.

"HOW DID YOU SLEEP, BABY GIRL," DOMINIQUE ASKS ONCE HE'S out of the shower and dressed.

"I slept like a log."

"I'm glad."

"I was a little surprised I slept through you buying all of this stuff."

"I had help from Kate and Jackson," he answers.

"That was very nice of them."

"Yeah. They were a huge help. We need to talk."

Uh oh, something's wrong. What happened since last night? I try racking my brain, but nothing comes to mind. I was out of it when we made it here to the hotel. "What is it?" I ask cautiously.

"The shooting. It was my fault."

"How?" I ask incredulously. "What do you mean?"

"The other night, I told Ethan we would be home alone, and Lucas was staying at a friend's house. We went out for drinks, and I knew something was up, but I never fathom he was involved with trying to kill us."

I pause, speechless. Because fuck, what the fuck do I say to that. He put our lives in danger to prove himself right. And for what? "I almost killed our friend," I barely mention. "You... How could you do that?" I spit out. "How could you?"

Dominique approaches me, trying to wrap his arms around my waist, but I push him off. "No, damnit. Don't fucking touch me."

"Harper, please?" He begs.

"Why? What the fuck were you thinking? You should've told me. I could have helped or done something, anything."

"I know, I just didn't want to worry you, and the doc said—."

"Fuck what the doctor said. You caused more harm than good. I'm upset now, and I shouldn't be. You did this. All of this. Now Ethan is fighting for his life. We might not have a fucking job, and my twisted ass family is still out there. Trying to kill the both of us."

"No, Harper. They're not. I reached out to Lt. Hall. His team, SWAT, and the Community Response Team took your father, mother, and brother into custody three hours ago," he explains. But I can't hear a word. Not one word. I lost my train of reasoning seconds ago.

"I have to get out of here. Anywhere. I can't breathe. I need air," I feel dizzy and uneasy on my feet. But before I hit the ground, Dominique catches me in his arms, and once again, I slip into eternal bliss. Lately, my favorite place to be.

CHAPTER FORTY-ONE

DOMINIQUE

A MONTH LATER

I FUCKING FUCKED UP, and Harper has every right to be pissed. She's right; I put both our lives in danger. I kept the most important information from her and now look, I haven't spoken to her in a month.

She refuses to take any of my calls or text messages. She just left, and I didn't bother following her because I'm a fucking coward.

After she left the hospital for a third time... I can't even fathom the torment I've put her through. Katie told me she still hasn't returned home, and we both are still on Admin leave.

Lucas and I are still at the JW, hoping and wishing Harper would return. I didn't have the heart to explain to him what had happened. I'm a fucking coward, and I deserve all the fucking misery God throws my way.

I should have told her. All she wanted was for me to be one hundred with her like I promised, and I fucked it up.

Lucas is fast asleep when I hear a knock on the door. I contemplate whether I should answer it until I hear Jackson's voice on the other side.

Who would have thought, us becoming close and shit? After the fucking débâcle with Ethan trying to kill Harper and me, Jackson became trustworthy. He and Katie have been checking on me every couple of days. Probably making sure I haven't hung myself in the bathroom.

I go to answer the door, and not only do I find Jackson at the door, but Ethan is also there.

"What the fuck," I spit out.

"Hear him out," Jackson urges. "It took a lot for him to come here."

"I bet it fucking did," I spit out.

"I'm sorry, man. For everything."

"You're fucking sorry. I've lost everything, and you're fucking sorry?" I ask incredulously. "Is this a fucking joke?"

"I know I don't deserve your forgiveness. I don't deserve anything, but I wanted to let you know what really happened. I can at least offer that much."

"You had ample time to come to me. I don't give two fucks what you got to say to me. Get the fuck out of my sight before I forget who the fuck I am."

I then slam the fucking door. What the fuck?

I need a fucking drink now! Hell, that's been my drug of choice these days. Ain't got nothing else to fucking do with my time.

I don't even bother pouring a glass. Instead, I drink straight from the bottle, again drinking myself into a fucking stupor.

CHAPTER FORTY-TWO

HARPER

I WAKE UP CRYING, and I go to sleep crying every night. After leaving the hospital, I couldn't manage to see Dominique or speak to him. So, I decided to stay at Katie's for now.

I was too exhausted to even care anymore. When I say I've lost everything, I mean everything. My world crashed the day my mother left me and burned the day Dominique betrayed me.

There's nothing he can say to me to make up for what he did, nothing.

I hear a knock on the bedroom door moments later, but of course, I don't bother budging. So, Katie being Katie, enters the room anyways.

"Harper, I'm coming in whether you like it or not."

"Ugh, leave me alone, Katie. I don't want to be bothered."

"And you know I don't give a shit. So you need to get your ass up. I've let you wallow in self-pity for a fucking month now."

"Katie, please."

"No, Harper. I love you, and I can't watch you do this to yourself."

She rips the curtains open, shedding light into the room, causing me to throw the blankets over my head.

"Oh, no, you don't," slinging the covers off me.

"Damnit!"

I sit up in bed, livid as shit right now, but Katie is doing me a huge favor because I don't have the strength to deal with my home right now. Our home...

And then the waterworks start once again. Every time I think of him, I start to drain my tear ducts. And I can't stop the madness even if I wanted to.

This is why I don't get attached. This is why I fuck and keep it moving. Damnit, I'm such an idiot.

"Now, this is what's going to happen," Katie begins with her threats. "You're going to get your ass up, take a shower, because face it, you stink, and you're going to go get your man back. You'll hear him out, listen, and not talk over him."

"And if I don't?" I challenge.

"Then I'm putting your ass out of my house. You have the best thing happening to you with him and Lucas, and you say fuck it all to hell?"

"He almost had us killed. How am I supposed to forgive that?"

"He didn't tell Ethan to come shoot up your house and try to kill you. That was Ethan's doing. And your family, well, you can't choose your family, and you know that."

"But he kept it from me."

"And you never kept anything from him?" She challenges. Damnit. I hate it when she's right. She's so fucking annoying. "You can't answer, can you?"

"No, I can't!"

"Then you need to forgive him and do it now. But get your shit together first."

"Fine. You're right, but I don't have to like it."

"No one said you did."

"Enough about me. Where's Jackson? I haven't seen him in a while."

"We're taking a break?"

"Oh, really. Pot, meet kettle black."

"It's not like that. He's been listening to rumors spreading through the precinct and never came to me to ask if they were true."

"What rumors? I didn't hear any rumors."

I walk into the closet and grab a pair of jeans and a tank with a long cozy cardigan. It's still a little cold out due to it being January. I practically slept straight through Christmas.

"Sweetie, you weren't in the precinct when they started or surfaced hard."

"Okay, but was it that bad to break up over?"

"Yeah. You remember I told you about my stripper days and having to make ends meet with school and everything?"

"Yeah, so?"

"Well, apparently, there's a video of me fucking someone at the strip club."

"What?"

"Yeah, and that's not it; according to the rumors, I've fucked my way through the entire department to get on the department because there's no way they would hire a prostitute."

"Oh my gosh. I had no idea this was happening. I could have helped you or stopped the shit from spreading like that."

"Please, you were knee-deep in your own drama. Hell, you almost died twice and are still here to tell about it."

"Yeah, but you're my friend. I should've been there for you. At least I could have knocked some sense into Jackson."

"Well, he's a true rich White boy. Can't possibly turn a hoe into a housewife and certainly can't bring her to meet mommy dearest and daddy."

"Well, I'm still rooting for y'all. Y'all are the cutest couple."

"I just wish he came to me. I would have given him the whole story."

"I know you would've."

"Enough about me. Get in the shower. We're leaving in an hour to fix this shit."

"Yes, ma'am."

CHAPTER FORTY-THREE

DOMINIQUE

I FINALLY GAVE in and decided to check out of the hotel. I found Lucas and me a four-bedroom home to purchase. Staying in this hotel will break me eventually, and it's time for us to find something of our own anyways.

I used the money I saved up by staying with Harper, and someday, when things calm down, I'll thank her for everything she has done for us.

She changed our lives, and I'm forever debited to her.

"Lucas, start packing your thing. We have to head out in an hour."

"Are we going back to Harper's?"

"No, we're not. We have a new home, and you'll have your own room and a gaming room. How does that sound?"

"I want to go back to Harper's." So do I. So do I.

He eventually gives in and stomps back to the room, letting me know he's not happy at all.

A couple of minutes later, I hear a knock on the door. It must be the luggage guy. I called about an hour ago to have someone assist us with our bags. We've accumulated a lot in the past month and a half.

I open the door, and at first, I have to do a double take because my eyes must be deceiving me, "Harper," I manage to say after several moments of hoping this isn't a dream. She's actually here? I ask myself, because this can't be real. She can't be here. Can she?

"Are you going to let us in?" She asks.

"Us?"

"Katie and me? She taking Lucas to Leopold's for ice cream while we talk."

"Yes, sorry. Of course, you can come in," opening the door wider for both of them. "Jackson?"

"Listen, don't bring up his name. Ever. Around me. Got it?" Katie demands.

"Yeah. Got it."

"Lucas, Auntie Katie wants to have a date with her favorite man," Katie singsongs through the room.

"Auntie Katie," Lucas screams, running full speed into her arms.

"High five," Katie holds her hand up to Lucas.

"Ms. Harper, you came," Lucas exclaims.

"Yes, buddy. I've missed you," Harper wraps her arms around Lucas, squeezing him tight.

"I've missed you too," he states heartfeltly.

He whispers something in her ear that I can't hear, and she bursts out laughing. God, that laugh will bring any man in earshot to their knees.

She then stands, "Can me and your dad talk a little while you hang out with Auntie Katie," she asks Lucas, ignoring me altogether.

"Absolutely! Take your time. You're going to need it," states matter-factly.

"And with that, we're leaving. Come on, little man. How about we hit up the Savannah Sweets store and then Leopold's for ice cream," Katie asks as they walk out the door, allowing it to swing shut behind them.

"So, can I get you a drink or something, anything?"

"Yes, I'll take a glass of wine and some Lay's potato chips," she states.

Weird combination, but who am I to judge. She's finally here.

"Coming right up."

I fix her a glass of wine and me a beer. I drank enough whiskey to last me a lifetime.

"Here," handing her the chips and the glass.

"Thank you,"

"Dominique—?"

"Harper—?"

"You first," she offers. Here goes nothing.

"Harper, I'm terribly sorry. I never meant to hurt you or put your life in danger. But I knew if I kept giving you bad news, it would land you in the hospital, and I couldn't fathom seeing you like that again. It nearly broke me."

"I know, Dom. I know you only did it to help, and you can't be responsible for what Ethan does, and I know that now. I've spent my entire life wondering why all of this shit happened to me, and I finally realized I can't choose my family, but I can choose the people I bring into my life, and ever since I've joined the department, I have a sense of belonging. Alpha watch is my family, and I don't know where I'd be without you, Lucas, Katie, and everyone else on the watch. I love you, Dom."

"Oh, God. I am so glad to hear that. I love you too, baby girl. I love you too."

I yank her into my lap, causing her to yelp. I then pull her mouth on mine, devouring her lips, taking from her what I've dreamt of for the past month. I've jacked off to her pictures, needing more than just a hand job, but the warmth of her sweet pussy.

I rip her clothes completely off, leaving a trail of shredded articles on the floor. Fuck it, I'll buy her more. I then flip her onto the couch, and I slide down on the floor to my knees, taking her pussy into my mouth. I fucking eat her out, causing her to come hard into my mouth. She moans so softly, it give me life, something I've craved; something I've been missing far too long. I take my jeans off, pick her up, and hold her against the wall, forcing her to wrap her legs around me. I shove my dick inside of her, and just the moans and cries from her pretty fuck-able mouth, it makes my legs turn into mush.

I fuck her hard and rough, and I still can't get enough of her. But, God, I love this woman, and I promise to make her the happiest woman alive, and that's a promise I intend to keep.

I feel her reaching her climax by gripping my dick for dear life. Then, finally, I don't think I can hold on any longer before I explode into her fat sweet pussy.

We're both out of breath as I guide down to the floor, turning so my back is against the wall and she cradling in my lap. She lays her head on my chest, and I feel our hearts racing.

"I love you, baby girl," kissing her forehead.

"I love you too."

EPILOGUE

HARPER

ONE YEAR LATER

IT'S BEEN a hell of a year, but with Dom by my side, I've overcome all obstacles thrown my way.

Dom and I returned to full duty after IA determined that we weren't responsible for all the shootings and assaults against us.

But, they made some changes around the precinct. Our entire watch has been divided into the other watches. Something about we had too many issues and needed to break up the monotony. Whatever. I'm just glad to be back to work.

My parents and brother's trial begins in the summer, and I've opted not to talk with them or ask them why. I don't care anymore. They aren't a part of my life. Hell, they never were. Besides, I'll see them in court, making sure those assholes rot in hell.

As for the money my dad left me, I'm creating a life with Dom and Lucas. A life I've always deserved. I regularly donate to the local women's shelter and foster homes for children.

And guess what? Dom and I adopted the cutest little girl. She was left at a fire station when we were working one night, and we instantly fell in love with her. So after a year of proving that we would be great parents without being married, we brought her home last week.

She has changed our lives, and I couldn't be happier with our little family. A family we created together, and I promise to be the best parent I know I can be to my children, Lucas and Clementine.

Lucas and Clementine are playing on the floor while I cook dinner. Dom is at work and should be home any minute now. I want to have the steaks and potatoes ready when he gets here.

I hear the door chime a few minutes later and am greeted by my handsome boyfriend. But wait, he has something in his arms.

Oh my goodness, it's a puppy, a toy poodle. He's so cute, with a bowtie around his neck and the color of midnight black.

"Oh my, what do we have here?" I approach Dom slowly.

"Happy birthday, baby girl. I know you've always wanted a toy poodle, and I finally found one."

"He's so precious. Can I hold him?"

"Yes, of course."

He hands me the poodle, and I wrap my arms gently around him, cradling him in my arms. I hold him in front of me and notice something dangling from his neck.

"Oh my gosh, Dom?" I look up with tears in my eyes.

With Clementine in his arms, Dom and Lucas get down on one knee. I can barely see with the droplets clouding my vision. I'm so overwhelmed with joy that I don't hear a word they are saying.

"Hun, sorry. I didn't hear you."

"Harper Madelyn Bradshaw, will you marry me?"

"Yes. Of course, I will."

He rises from his knees, takes the ring off the poodle, and places it on my finger. I then feel Lucas wrap his arms around my legs and Clementine blowing spit bubbles as Dom kisses me like the very first time he laid eyes on me.

How so much has changed in the past two years, and I wouldn't have it any other way...

ALSO BY NICOLETTE JOHNSON

Don't forget to indulge in all volumes of the *Handcuffed* Series:

Handcuffed

Shackled

Bounded

Entangled

Coming Soon:

Savannah's Finest Series:

Book II

Bravo Watch

Let me know how you like the series thus far

Facebook @authornicolettejohnson

Twitter @PenNicoletteJo

Instagram @authornicolette

www.authornicolettejohnson.com